Amanda Lee ♡
Muldrew

319 Rogers RD.

Dear America

The Diary of Deliverance Trembley, Witness to the Salem Witch Trials

I Walk in Dread

LISA ROWE FRAUSTINO

SCHOLASTIC INC. • NEW YORK

To my daughter, Daisy Fraustino

Copyright © 2004 by Lisa Rowe Fraustino

The Library of Congress has cataloged the earlier hardcover edition as follows:
Fraustino, Lisa Rowe. I walk in dread : the diary of Deliverance Trembley, witness to the Salem
witch trials / by Lisa Rowe Fraustino. — 1st ed. p. cm. — (Dear America) Summary: Twelve-
year-old Deliverance Trembley writes in her diary about the fears and doubts that arise during
the 1692 witch hunt and trials in Salem Village, Massachusetts, especially when her pious
friend, Goody Corey, is condemned as a witch. ISBN 0-439-24973-2 1. Trials (Witchcraft)—
Massachusetts—Salem—Juvenile fiction. [1. Trials (Witchcraft)—Fiction. 2. Witchcraft—Fiction.
3. Puritans—Fiction. 4. Prejudices—Fiction. 5. Sisters—Fiction. 6. Salem (Mass.)—History—
Colonial period, ca. 1600–1775—Fiction. 7. Diaries—Fiction.] I. Title. II. Series. PZ7.F8655Iae
2004 [Fic]—dc22   2004005606

This edition ISBN 978-0-545-31165-6

10 9 8 7 6 5 4 3 2 1   11 12 13 14 15

The text type was set in ITC Legacy Serif.
The display type was set in PastonchiMT.
Book design by Kevin Callahan

Printed in the U.S.A. 23
This edition first printing, September 2011

Massachusetts Bay Colony

1691

To Ye Who Holds This Book:

If you are able to read these words, I beg you read no more. This book is merely a private account of my days, never meant for the eyes of others. If by some reason of God's design I am gone from Salem Farms and the book cannot be returned to me, pray toss it into the flames. I am the Lord's faithful servant,

Deliverance Trembley

Tuesday ye 29th of December, 1691

Thank You, dear Lord, for causing me to trip over a hen this morning! You sent the apples flying out of my apron and rolling under the cabinet. Reaching for them my hand found something stuck under the back edge of the cabinet, holding it steady. The object did not feel like wood, and I felt curious. I called to Mem to ask her to help me move the cupboard, but in answer she only coughed. My sister lay abed all morning complaining of her breathing, as she typically does when there is work to be done. Yesterday the Widow Holten brought a bag of wool to spin into thread.

Never mind, with a sickly sister I am used to fending for myself. I braced my legs, hoisted the edge of the cupboard away from the wall, and gasped at the sight:

A book!

A book with black leather binding, caked with dust, too thick to be a Psalm book or a pamphlet, too thin to be the Gospel. It gave me such a shock that I near fainted. Why would such a fine volume be found in mine uncle's house? He does not know 2 from Z, and he sees no use for reading anything but the Bible.

He once caught me reading while I was at the spinning wheel. I argued that I can read and spin at the same time while still producing more and better thread than Mem; and this be the God's honest truth. But that mattered not to mine uncle. It did not even matter that I was reading a worthy book that was being passed around the whole Village after the Reverend Parris himself spoke of it in a sermon. No, Uncle Razor Strap whipped me full sore, anyway. I am glad he has sneaked away on a whaling ship and left us alone these weeks!

So: Here I stand witness to a secret book, cleverly hidden away, and all I can wonder is one thing. Am I looking at a mere prop for a crooked cabinet, or am I looking at the Devil's Book, where he maketh his witches sign their names in blood? Is mine uncle a wizard?

I never did hear him praise the Devil; however, one Sabbath morning after he broke the ice in the bowl to wash his face, I did hear him curse. "If God hath already predestined us all to heaven or hell, I see no reason to freeze my arse off on a hard bench all day!" While Mem and I huddled in the unheated Meeting House for five never-ending hours with muffs around our hands and the dog curled around our feet for warmth, our uncle went ice fishing. We did more shivering than listening. He carried home a string of trout and the smell of rum.

Mine uncle behaves more like a sinner than a wizard. Yet, it is well known that witches can live in secret among us, working the Devil's harm. Why, there were eleven of them accused in Hartford some years ago, and everyone knows what happened to the Goodwin children of Boston in 1688.

They fell into the most terrible fits and visions that did not end until the witch who was tormenting them was found and put to death. Could mine own uncle be off doing the Devil's work at this very moment, rather than fishing for whales as he had told us? What horror!

I did not dare touch the book with my bare fingers lest evil be given a straight path to my heart. Yet, I could not resist looking inside. It was a book, after all, and except for the Lord Himself there is nothing I love more. Besides, if mine uncle ever sold his soul to the Devil, it would be my Christian duty to tell the Reverend Parris.

Trembling from head to foot, heart pounding, I lifted the black leather cover with the toe of my shoe.

And laughed out loud!

For it was no book of the Devil filled with witches' names, but a book with blank pages! My father had one like it to keep his accounts, God rest him. Now I may keep an account of my days, as I used to do before our uncle came to Hartford and took us off the hands of the dear Widow Ruste, who taught me to read and write and spin and make butter and soap. Would that he left us there; she would have kept us, but our father's will declared his brother our guardian, and our mother died when I was three, so there was no choice in the matter.

I can write no more today. I must hide the book before Mem returns from trading eggs. It amazes me how she always gets her wind back just in time to make a deal with the neighbors! Mem cannot read, but she knows her name when she sees it, and the last time I kept a diary she constantly badgered me to read aloud the parts about her. Mem never loses an argument. This time I wish to complain about her in peace! I hope she brings home a soup bone with some meat on it. The one thing I miss about our uncle is his hunting.

As for him, he shall not notice that the book is gone, unless God causes him to fall and lose his apples from his apron. I made the cabinet level with a chunk of wood. And now I must find a safe hiding place.

My Book and Heart
Shall never part.

Wednesday ye 30th of December, 1691

My book stays safe in the root cellar, where Mem never goes. The main crop of this little farm is an orchard, and she always makes me go for the apples when people come to trade. She says she cannot breathe in the root cellar. The place is small and dark and smells of dirt. I think the place is snug and comforting. Our father taught us to hide in the root cellar if our house was ever attacked, and it was, and we did, but today I am telling of my book and mine uncle.

He will not find the book, for it is hidden as if invisible, in a space behind a rock. Keeping the book a secret from our uncle is only fitting, since he left us guarding a secret of his own, and here it is: The neighbors are forbidden to discover that he has gone away! Mem and I must keep up appearances of his presence here in Salem Farms. He does not want it known that we are two girls alone without a man to support and protect us. Mem is seventeen years of age, and I am twelve.

Our brother, Benjamin, is twenty. He will finish his tour with the militia in time to help with the spring planting. For now, though, Mem and I are on our own to tend the animals and trade our eggs and apples. We are well able to take care of ourselves; that is not the problem. The problem is the Villagers, who would not approve, and might condemn our uncle, and remove us from his care.

Mem demanded to know if he was asking us to lie.

"Of course not," our uncle replied. "Lying is an abomination unto the Lord."

I wanted to know what we should say if anyone asks where he is.

"That I am working. That is no lie."

But what if anyone asks where he is working?

"Do I tell you my whereabouts every moment of the day? No. I could be logging to the west, I could be trapping to the north, I could be whaling off New Bedford, for all you know."

We had to laugh at that! For we finally understood what he was asking us to do: conceal the facts in truth, so as not to sin. At first I was unsure whether this nimbleness of wording would count as honesty. God knows the sins in our hearts, even if they do not travel up the throat. However, I now believe that the Lord does not disapprove. If He did, our lips would be covered with sores by now to show the world we had sinned with our mouths.

And what if anyone asks when our uncle will be home? We do not know. He did not tell us. It could be at any moment. And he could have been home at any moment for several weeks now.

When he does return, he expects to have enough money in his pockets to buy this little farm instead of rent it, and he wants to build a cider mill. As a landowner he will rise greatly in status. He will be able to join the church (should he ever be moved by the grace of God to do so). He will also be eligible to vote on town matters. I hope the seating committee will assign Mem and me to a pew with the unmarried girls at the Meeting House. We never know what folk will come sit next to us in the free area. One day that homeless wretch Sarah Goode sat by me and stunk so bad of her vile pipe that I could hardly hear the sermon.

And so, having mastered the art of hiding the truth while speaking no lies, we live each day as if we expect our uncle home for supper.

For turkey braised
The Lord be praised.

Thursday ye 31st of December, 1691
Oh, how I enjoy these days being left alone without Uncle Razor Strap telling me what to do! If

Mem and I had been abandoned for weeks on end when we lived on the frontier in Maine, I would have been terrified. Here, though, there is little to fear.

No wolves stalking us on a walk to the neighbor's.

No bears come to supper.

No Wabanakis rushing out of the trees to take captives.

Mem and our three brothers were all born in Maine. Only I, the youngest, was born in Connecticut. The family took refuge with our mother's cousin, the Widow Ruste, in Hartford during King Philip's War. Our father waited until he felt the peace was secure before returning Eastward. I remember the long journey on the lap of my new stepmother, and all the hope we felt for our future. Little did we know how short the peace would be . . . how short many things would be. Oh, I do not wish to think of this!

For her eggs, Mem brought home a few ounces of dried meat and a pound of gossip. Most of it is old news but new to us. Though her breathing seldom keeps Mem home, the weather often does. We have missed many Lecture Days and Sabbaths because of snow. I dearly hope we do not get snowed in again this Sunday. I suppose we shall hear again that the Reverend Parris has barely enough firewood to last the day. This has frequently been the case since November. He has not been paid his salary in months, and repeatedly petitions the churchmen to honor his contract.

Mem reported that on the 18th John Hadlock came to town to collect his shillings. Francis Nurse is paying Hadlock to take the place of his youngest son in the militia. Hadlock is serving Eastward in Maine with our Benjamin. God be praised, Hadlock left word that Ben is well. I do not see why some men have to fight over and over until they lose their lives while others get to stay at home, but it is not my place to question the Lord's will. Perhaps God wants to keep the Nurse boy here because he has a young wife and baby.

The selectmen abated the Widow Shafflin's taxes again, her man being gone and sickness in her family. Her husband died of smallpox, and her children are taken with it. News of this brought me to tears with memories of my father and brothers. After all of their struggles to tame the frontier and battle the French and Indians, it was the pox that got them. It is times like these when I feel that Mem and I are truly alone.

Time cuts down all
Both great and small.

Friday ye 1st of January, 1691

Remembrance Trembley, how can you snore the
night away while mine eyes are stuck wide open
in fear of what evil you may have tempted to this
house!

This morning the dog set to barking and the
chickens set to squawking, telling us someone
was coming to the door. Even though Mem had
spent the past hour coughing and wheezing over
the Widow's work, she jumped up to pull the knot
out of the wall next to the door and peek through
the hole. The knot-hole spyglass is a clever trick
our uncle designed for our security. We are not to
go near the windows.

"It's Susannah come for apples!" Mem said.
Mem and Susannah Sheldon were both born
in Maine, and that alone made them fast friends.
Mem pulled the bar from the door and latched
on to Susannah in a tearful embrace. It was the
first time they had seen each other since the death
of Susannah's father. He fell and cut his knee.
The sore festered, and two weeks later he was

gone. How sad! He had lived through far worse.

Through the door I noticed how the walking path split like a Y through the deep snow to the road and the barn. The gray sky promised to spit more snow. A bitter gust of wind raced across the floor like rats off a ship, through the holes in the bottoms of my shoes and straight up my bones to my teeth. Careless girls! Even with the door shut the air is barely warmer inside than out!

"If the chickens take a chilling, they will not lay," I said, and pushed past Mem and Susannah to close the door.

By the time the two girls had finished their bawling, I had filled Susannah's basket with apples and was back to my spinning. They sat at the table to fret over their uncertain futures. So many young men of New England have lost their lives in the wars, and so many are off fighting now, that the Village is overflowing with unmarried girls with no prospects. I soon became bored with listening to their whining, and began humming and singing to the chickens, who like my voice. Our father taught us that a calm voice will soothe any beast, and I believe my Psalms do keep the eggs coming.

Suddenly the song was startled out of me by a scream from across the room. The chickens clucked, the cat howled, the dog barked. It was a frightful commotion, and I leaped to my feet to see what was wrong.

Susannah stood leaning on the tableboard with her knuckles white, all the color drained from her cheeks, her terrified eyes staring into a glass of water. The water was cloudy with almost invisible shapes, and a cloudy film settled on the bottom. "What is this?" I said. A suspicion was creeping into my mind, but I did not want to believe my sister would take part in any such thing.

"A coffin!" Susannah whispered, in a voice that rose hackles on the back of my neck. My suspicion was correct: The girls were fortune-telling! They had made a venus glass—an egg dropped in water—to tell them the trade of Susannah's future sweetheart.

How dare they! "Have you not paid attention in church? Magic of any kind, be it black or white, is of the Devil!"

"Oh, go sing to yourself," Mem said, rolling her eyes at me. "It is just a game for sport. There is no more evil in this glass than there is in a cloudy sky. Girls have been doing this sort of thing forever."

Susannah was still staring, yet not seeing. She seemed lost in a world behind her eyes. Mem grabbed her hand and tugged it playfully. "Look again," she said. "Now it looks like a tree. Your husband will be a carpenter."

It mattered not to me what the shape foretold. I was disgusted. "Mem, I cannot believe you wasted an egg for this," I said. And she risked losing her soul, too, but I did not do her the favor of saying so, after being insulted.

Susannah pulled herself from her daze and asked to speak with our uncle. Her mother needs a man to help her with some heavy labor. Mem sighed deeply, and looked tired. Concealing the truth in facts takes near as much effort as spinning wool. "Lately his work has taken him away from the Village every day. Perhaps your mother should ask someone else?"

As soon as Susannah left, I put on my coat. The Reverend Parris had to hear what sorcery the foolish girls had performed! He would know how to mend the damage to their souls.

Mem grabbed my arm and argued me out of going to the Reverend. He would want to speak to our uncle. If he discovered we were two girls alone, there was no telling what would happen.

My coat came off only on the condition that

Mem repent her sin. She did spend the evening in prayer, but I could tell she did it to humor me, not to humble herself before the Lord. Hence I remain full of fear, and ye, my dear book, have yet another secret to keep.

Saturday ye 2nd of January, 1691/2

Snow prickled my cheeks on the way in from tending the barn animals this morning. We have no need for snow on top of snow. Pray it is only a flurry.

Noon . . .

Two inches dropped already. Pray it is only a squall. I am going to drag Mem out of bed and make her shovel. It is her turn to empty the slop bucket, too.

Afternoon . . .

The sky outside the window is a wall of white. Pray the blizzard blows over quickly, so I can clear the paths before bed and go to the Meeting House in the morning. Have given up on getting Mem to shovel, because she offered to make the supper and she is a better cook than I am. However, I reminded her that just as God knows the number of hairs on her head, I know the number of chickens in the loft. A braised hen cannot lay eggs.

Dusk . . .

Have given up on shoveling. Pray the blizzard passes in the night and does not spend tomorrow laying down more. We will be a week digging out from under it! Mem made a savory stew with vegetables and the last of the dried meat, and she baked an apple pie that melted in my mouth and makes me look forward to breakfast.

January ye 3rd, the Sabbath

Lord, I would rather be at the Meeting House this moment, but the roads are well over my knees in snow. This book is such a pleasure to me that I hope You will not count my writing as labor on Thy day of rest.

Wind blasted down the chimney last night and rattled the shutters with driving snow. Despite the blizzard the dog barked, and there came a knock at the door. My heart fluttered with gladness, thinking it must be our uncle. After all the shoveling I was in the mood to miss him. Mem called loudly, "Who is there?"

Not our uncle. Strangers! "Jones Darcy Cooper

and son, weary travelers from Haver'il, stuck on the road and in need of shelter."

We could not in good Christian faith leave them stranded out in the storm. We opened the door, and in two snowmen tumbled. Uttering thanks, they stomped their feet, peeled back their hoods, and made a beeline for the hearth to warm their hands. With his coat open the father's scarlet waistcoat showed. It was neat as new and had golden buttons. Weary travelers, but not poor ones!

Mem smiled, giving me the elbow in the ribs, meaning she finds a fellow handsome. Handsome? I suppose he is, if one likes tall men who are wide in the shoulders, with a full head of hair, and no pockmarks on their faces. The son, however, is the ugliest boy I ever laid eyes on. He has scarred skin and a short, crooked leg. He does have his father's unusual nose—long and arched, with a bump just before the tip turns up—but it looks much better on the father.

Handsome Mr. Cooper surveyed our two rooms with a look of chagrin. "We are not at John Proctor's." Mr. Proctor and his wife, Elizabeth, operate a tavern for travelers down a road near here. "No," Mem said. "You are at the Trembleys'. I am

Remembrance, and this is my sister, Deliverance."

Mr. Cooper's face took on a grim look and he said, "My senses were confounded by the snow. We shall have to continue on our way. What objects are there along the road to help us find the path, Goodwife Trembley?"

Mem blushed at his address and tossed her head back in a soft laugh. We should have donned our bonnets before we opened the door! Her loose curls bounced and gleamed in the firelight. "I am not married, good Sir," she said.

The good Sir apologized for the presumption, and looked her all up and down like a cow he was buying! In her shameful place I would have cast mine eyes to the floor, but Mem met his gaze evenly. I think she enjoyed his attention!

The quiet son touched his father's arm, and gulped before he spoke. Words seemed to struggle to get off of his tongue. I had trouble following his meaning. "Father, it would be folly to push the horses any farther in this storm."

Listening to him stutter is painful, yet he has a pleasant tone to his voice. Methinks the hens would like to hear him hum. He has bright eyes, too, and wears half a smile. I wondered if he has a sweetheart, but I did not ask. I did not want him to think I wish to be his sweetheart. I have no desire for one.

"I am afraid my son is correct," Mr. Cooper said. "We are going to have to prevail upon you good people for room and board. Could I speak to your father?"

Mem was gazing up at him, her tongue tied and her eyes soft and smitten, God help us. "Our father is with the Lord," I said. "This is our uncle's house."

"Then will you please fetch your uncle?" said Mr. Cooper.

"I am afraid our uncle did not come back from his work today," I said. "For all we know, he may be knocking on the door of your house looking for shelter." After a pause, handsome Mr. Cooper laughed, and so did his ugly son. What a beautiful laugh ugly Mr. Cooper has! His voice filled the room like the music of a brook.

Handsome Mr. Cooper's brow furrowed. "What an uncomfortable situation!" he said. "Two girls unchaperoned, and strange men in the house. We must travel on, Son." His voice carried his doubt. I worried for their safety.

Travel in snow
In wind don't go.

Mem found her tongue now. "No, no, we will not hear of it! You must get your horses into the barn immediately, not push them on through the blizzard. You have no choice but to stay here, Mr. Cooper. And you must be hungry!"

Handsome Mr. Cooper looked into the fire, gave the matter thought, and nodded. "All right. If you would be so kind as to allow us, we would be grateful to take some supper, and stay in the barn for the night."

The barn! With the animals and the outhouse? The place had not been mucked out in days, the weather being so miserable. It would be dark and damp and cold, as well as smelly. Mem and I both insisted they stay in the house, where it is not so freezing cold, but they insisted that doing so would not be seemly. So the barn is where they slept, and the barn is where they are this very moment, going at the muck, though it be a sin to work on Sunday, and Mem is *helping* them (cough, cough). Now I must fix them dinner.

Monday ye 4th of January

The Coopers still cannot travel. The roads are heaped with snow past a horse's knees, and the wind is still whipping. We have all prayed that God will stop the wind and allow the sun to open the roads. We have also prayed for the safe return of our uncle.

From now on I will muck and Mem will cook. While I was burning the corn bread, Mem near coughed her head off until the men sent her inside. Mr. Cooper and Darcy do not seem to think her lazy at all! (The ugly son told us that his father is *Mister* Cooper, and we should call him Darcy.) Darcy told us one of his brothers cannot breathe easily when he has to work in the cold. This brother also has trouble breathing if he sleeps on a goose-down mattress, or if the cat sits on his lap, or if he has to sweep the barn. Sounds to me that if the boy is not lazy, then he has been bewitched! But the Coopers just think wheezy is the way God made him.

Darcy has eight younger brothers and sisters. The boy who cannot breathe is somewhere in the middle. Imagine it! Nine living children from the same two parents! With wet eyes he told us that their mother passed from this earth a year ago. (Mem expressed sympathy, but I could tell she was pleased to hear that Mr. Cooper has no wife.)

The Coopers are so amply blessed by God's providence, they are clearly among His Elect. They trade in barrels, which they manufacture in Haver'il. They own hundreds of wooded acres and operate their own sawmill and forge. They keep a shop in Haver'il and also deliver barrels to merchants and traders along the coast. Darcy as the eldest is learning from his father to run all aspects of the business. The next brother, Adam, operates the sawmill. After Adam, Darcy has a sister, Mehitabel, who runs the shop. Mehitabel is married to the blacksmith, who operates the forge. The rest of the children are still in school. School! How I would love to go!

To hear the stories Mr. Cooper tells of his family, I think they must all be very smart and industrious. Darcy's little sister Rebecca could already say her alphabet and most of her catechism at age two years. Now at age three she can already read, and she loves to count the fleas and ticks as she picks them off the pets. Mem made me blush when she told them I was the same way as a young child. Then I blushed even more when she said I used to count her fingers and somehow get to twelve!

Praise God, cooking does not make Mem cough! Today she has filled the house with good smells that will soon fill our mouths with good tastes and our bellies with good meat. The Coopers brought in from their wagon a chunk of corned beef. She rinsed it in cold water, placed it in a kettle, and is following this recipe:

• Cover with water and simmer one hour.
• Pour off the liquid and add boiling water to cover.
• Simmer another 3 hours. (That is where the corned beef is now, and so Mem is simmering in her bed . . . I mean snoring! The Coopers are outside working.)
• Add 6 white onions and 4 small turnips, and cook 30 minutes more.
• Add 6 carrots and 7 potatoes, and simmer 15 minutes.
• Add one head of cabbage cut in 6 pieces. (If you have it. We do not, but we have horseradish to serve with the boiled dinner.)
• Cook it all until tender.

One hour? Thirty minutes? How does Mem know? When I cook, boil turns to braise, simmer turns to scald, cream turns to curdle — and I never nap!

Tuesday ye 5th of January

The wind has died down. Now we are just waiting for the sun. The workhorses could travel through the snow today if they did not have to drag the sleigh with its heavy cargo. Mem attempted to convince the Coopers to leave the sleigh here and come back for it after the roads clear. (And then she would be sure to see *Mister* again.) This was one argument she could not win. However, she received two charming smiles for her efforts.

Darcy and his father kept themselves busy these two days chopping wood, oiling leather, sharpening tools, and grooming animals. They admiringly say that our uncle keeps a tight farm. They admire the convenient design of the outhouse he built in the barn. They also remarked on the clever knothole and the chicken coop in the loft. Our uncle made an artful design of neatly carved sticks to let the heat and light in without letting the hens out. Mem pointed out that our departed father made the cabinet and the two chairs, and they said the Trembleys come from talented stock!

After the day's work and supper, we gathered by the fire to pray for a long time. Then we again shared stories of our families until the candles burned down. Mr. Cooper loves to tell tales (and Mem clearly loves to watch him). He told how Darcy got his crooked leg from falling off a milk stool when he was small. His scars come from a pox he and Adam suffered as young children, before the other seven were born. Both survived!

I remarked that our father and brothers were not so blessed. They fell to the pox they brought home from the wars. Mr. Cooper said I should not take their suffering as a sign of God's punishment. The pox cannot tell a sinner from a saint, he said, and anyone who catches it is in for the battle of his life. In fact, God often gives His chosen people the greatest trials. Look at Job. Look at Jesus! Mr. Cooper is a kind man.

Then it was Mem's turn to tell tales. She puts me in mind of the Reverend Parris the way she can hold her listeners tight to her words. The Coopers leaned forward in their seats, their faces showing every proper emotion. They laughed when she told them how our three brothers once got in a brawl while tarring the roof in Maine, rolled off of the roof onto the ground, and kept on fighting. Mr. Cooper and Darcy crooned sympathy when she told of the fearful day when Ben, she, and I huddled in the root cellar while our stepmother bravely distracted the Indians from finding us. Our stepmother was taken captive, and as far as we knew she was still in Canada with them. I was too young to remember it for myself, yet Mem makes me feel as though her memories are my own.

Now the two men have put on snowshoes and taken a walk to see whether the neighbors have cleared the main roads yet. The Coopers do itch to get home to their family. Having them here makes my heart ache for the ones Mem and I have lost. Pray Lord protect and keep Benjamin safe from harm. And bring our uncle home soon!

Wednesday ye 6th of January
The Coopers have gone. They lost patience with the sun and took matters into their own hands. They rigged up a plow to be pulled by two horses, the other four following with the sleigh.

Mr. Cooper left a letter for our uncle, thanking him for the hospitality of his household. (We did not tell him our uncle cannot read.) Mr. Cooper said the next time he and Darcy pass through the area they will stop to meet our uncle. (We did not tell him our uncle might be whaling off the shores of New Bedford, for all we know.) We are to watch for the Coopers on Mondays, when they travel to; and on Saturdays, when they travel fro. They like to be home for the Sabbath.

Mem packed them a meal of corn bread and cheese, and an apple cake that sent them off smiling. It smelled so good, I wanted to travel to Haver'il with it.

Bah, all the better that they left. Had the storm kept them here any longer, we would have gone through the whole winter's worth of candles and cheese.

Thursday ye 7th of January

Mem can speak of nothing but Mr. Cooper. Mr. Cooper, Mr. Cooper, Mr. Cooper. She is convinced that Mr. Cooper intends to court her. All the time he was here he did treat her politely, and smile at her often, and praise her cooking, as did Darcy, and he did study her up and down when he heard she was not married. Still, I do not believe he could possibly have serious intentions.

Why would a businessman and landowner like him want a wife like Mem? With a large family to raise, would he not be more interested in finding someone older and more experienced in running a household? There are plenty enough widows from high families needing husbands. Mem is but the niece of a poor laborer. She cannot even read, and when there is work to be done, she can barely breathe enough to argue. Mr. Cooper needs a help-mate, not a help-eat!

Friday ye 8th of January

Today the sun came out, and then it rained. The snow has melted in half. Pray the warm weather holds and the rain does not turn white. I am eager to get out of this little house on Sunday and join the congregation in fellowship.

I have not been in the company of girls my age in weeks. Enough listening to Mem about sweethearts! It will be good to see Abigail Williams and Ann Putnam again, but I hope that foolish Hobbs girl will leave me alone. She used to live in Maine, too, and likes to think we are friends. We are not! She will do anything for attention. She is rude and unseemly to her parents and is not afraid of anything.

One time she came up to the group of girls while we were playing cratch-cradle, and told us she had met the Devil! He introduced himself to her in the Maine woods. My startled fingers missed a string when she claimed, "I sold myself body and soul to the old boy." Mercy Lewis pushed Hobbs away and said the little liar just saw an Indian. Mercy will not admit it, but I heard that she and Hobbs are related somehow.

Mem is eager to get out on Sunday, too. She can hardly wait to break the news of her beloved barrel-maker to Susannah.

Susannah!

God help me!

How could I have forgotten about the venus glass! I wonder if any evil has befallen her? I had better go pray.

Saturday ye 9th of January

> The moon gives light
> In time of night.

Last night the clouds blew over for a short time and allowed the full moon to shine down on the glazed snow. The frozen orchard seemed covered in jewels. The white rolling fields glittered with the grandeur of God. In that moment I felt as one with all creation. I felt like part of something too big and too beautiful to understand. Was that a moment of grace? Is that what it feels like to know one is among God's Elect? As I wondered, the clouds came roiling in and returned the world to darkness. Did that mean I am not one of His chosen few?

I went to bed feeling sore confused, and had a confusing dream. I was a Wabanaki girl long ago, long before the *Mayflower,* looking in awe at the full moon shining down upon the glittering earth, and feeling as one with all creation. The clouds covered the moon, and I went into my uncle's wigwam to sleep next to my sister in a bed of deerskin.

The dream surrounded me in peace while I was in it, but upon waking, my heart raced in my ribs. I was an Indian, a barbarous heathen, yet felt as holy as I have ever felt singing a Psalm! What could it mean? Have I sinned in my sleep? God save me.

I had better make sure nobody ever finds this book, else I wind up in the stocks on the Village green for blasphemy. Perhaps I will burn it, after the pages are full of words.

Monday ye 11th of January

The sun and rain have melted most of the snow, and thawed the roads, so that the horses and wagons have churned them to mud. On our walk to the Village yesterday, Mem and I made our way along the side of the road, trying to keep out of the mess by stepping on dead grass or clods of snow. However, the Reverend's niece Abigail Williams found use for the mud. She is ever filled with ideas for new things to do.

It being warm like spring outside, the young people went out of doors during the nooning. Abigail picked up a stick and drew her initials in the mud. It was her mark, she said. We girls should all be prepared to sign our own special marks on official documents, and not fall back on a simple *X* like ignorant folk. Thy mark should have a unique shape to show thy personality.

Hearing this, Mem let out a big round laugh and wanted to know why girls would ever need to do such a thing as sign our names. "Would ye have us brand our bread like cattle?"

The other girls looked sidelong at Abigail for her reaction, and saw her smiling, so they all laughed with Mem. Abigail handed the stick to Ann Putnam, saying, "Here be your branding iron." Abigail and Ann are forever whispering to each other and making sport, and when I see them, I suffer the sin of envy. Why do they not include me? I am their age. Like Ann, I have survived many siblings. Like Abigail, I am an orphan who lives with an uncle (if he would come home). Perhaps, I thought, this game would be my chance to win their friendship.

Ann tried many swoops and swirls and settled on a mark that looked like so:

Then she surveyed the excited faces to choose the next writer. My heart skipped with hopes that she would pass the stick to me. However, Ann handed the stick to Elizabeth Hubbard, who is seventeen, like Mem, and lives with Dr. Griggs and his wife, who is her aunt. She stepped up and drew a mark like this:

Again, my heart skipped. Elizabeth teased Mercy Lewis and Mary Walcott by holding the stick toward them and then pulling it back before giving it over to Mem. Mem! Who had scoffed at the idea! My heart curled with bitterness, God forgive me, and I hoped that she would embarrass herself.

Mem stepped up and drew an egg shape. Inside, she made two eyes crossed, and a mouth with a tongue sticking out. This was her mark!

The girls laughed and laughed! The ones who had not made their mark begged to have the stick next. The vile Hobbs girl tried to grab it, but Mercy kicked her ankles till she ran away. I stepped in front of Susannah to plead the loudest. Mem is my sister, after all. She tried to make me promise to empty the slop bucket for the rest of her unmarried life before she would give me the stick. I said I would promise not to tell the girls any of her secrets if she gave me the stick. And so she gave it to me, and I stepped up and took my turn in the mud.

Deliverance Trembley

As I wrote, the air grew heavy and silent. When I turned to witness their expressions, I expected to see only awe and admiration. Abigail and Ann would put their arms in mine and skip off to be a circle of three. Instead, I saw only the face of my sister rolling her eyes at me in disgust, and the backs of the other girls returning to the Meeting House.

"What did I do wrong?" I asked Mem, and she refused to answer.

"If you are so smart," she said, "then you should not need me to explain such a simple thing to you." Lord, I am not so smart. I do not understand.

Tuesday ye 12th of January

Perhaps God used the girls to punish me for wishing Mem ill in the game? I have repented of that, and hope the group will not shun me next week.

Even though snow and ice bound us into the house but a week ago, there is none left to thaw over the fire for our use. Yet we are still housebound. The rain and all the snow it melted have flooded out all the lowlands. The roads have liquefied. It feels like March without the hope of greens.

Mem and I are a miserable and thirsty pair.

We are out of fresh water. There is barely enough left in the bucket to boil the dinner, yet I refuse to fetch the water on top of all the rest I do. My shoes have both worn through at the big round bone beneath the fat toe. My lazy sister, whose shoes are like new, should be the one to trudge through the mud and flood to the common well. She will dry up like a beef jerky before I will shoulder those empty pails! It is vowed: I shalt not show my face at the well. Mem shall see that she is not the only stubborn Trembley around here!

Noon . . .

Dirty puddles are forming at the edges of the floor, seeping in through the walls where the water has pooled outside. As I sop them up with rags, the puddles tempt me to drink. However, I will not admit to Mem that I am thirsty. When she nags me to stop moping about ruining the girls' game and go fill the buckets, I say to her, "You know where the well is, Mistress Pining for Mr. Cooper."

Afternoon . . .

The animals are lowing with thirst. I have plugged my ears with wool and am going to lie down to sleep so I cannot hear them. Mem is bound to take pity and give up her stubbornness very soon.

Evening . . .

Dreamt that I was lying facedown in the shallows of the Ipswich River and gorging myself with water until my innards swelled like the udder of an unmilked cow. This is surely a message from the Lord that I must drink. I confess: I am not as stubborn as Mem. I will go fetch the water, though the road swallow my feet and chew up my shoes.

Wednesday ye 13th

On the way back from the well I saw that poor little waif Dorcas Goode tramping along the road toward the Village with her awful mother, out begging for food and shelter. Such is their life, eating the crumbs that people throw them, sleeping in barns with the animal dung and fleas. Folks say Sarah Goode is a witch and will curse the cows of anyone who turns her away. Folks also say that Sarah Goode was not always poor, that she actually came from a fine, wealthy family. However, only our All-Knowing Father in heaven would know that by looking at her. If not for the dirt holding them together, the stinking rags she wears would likely fall apart.

My pity for them soon turned to shame for myself. But for the grace of God, that could be Mem and me. Then my shame turned to fear. What if some evil has befallen our uncle and he does not return? Mem and I will be truly alone to find our way in the world. I was awash with regret for arguing with her over doing the work. I do not know what possessed me to do it, or to get so angry with her when she was chosen to write her mark in the mud. The Devil must have gotten into me. We have a roof over our heads and food in our stomachs. We should be grateful for God's providence, and beseech Him to continue it.

Upon return home I left my mud-soaked shoes by the door and asked Mem to join me in prayer. We sang our favorite Psalms by the firelight, and after we climbed in bed with our heated rocks I asked Mem to tell me stories about our mother. Mem cannot read or write, but she can talk a pretty picture. Her stories make our mother come alive in my imagination: her soft voice, her quick laugh, her kind teachings. It was she who taught Mem to cook. I fell asleep with the image of my mother nursing me, while little Mem turned the cakes on the pan.

This morning, without a word, Mem got up and went to fetch water.

Thursday ye 14th

The Widow Holten came to get her wool thread today, and to speak with our uncle about bringing her a wagon of hardwood chopped small for cooking. We told her he was out about at work, we did not know where. She asked when he would return. She is near out of wood and would like to see him soon.

Mem elbowed me in the ribs. She thinks the Widow Holten is sweet on our uncle. I cannot imagine anyone being sweet on our uncle. He only washes his face for Sunday Meeting, and does not believe in changing his clothes unless they need mending. But Mem may be right. The Widow does get him to do this, that, and the other thing even though she has relatives nearby.

We informed her that our uncle never tells us when he will be home. He might have sailed back to England to see the king and Increase Mather, for all we knew. At this, she laughed. The Reverend Increase Mather has been in England for many months trying to convince the king to restore the charter. We make jokes to lighten our worries. The charter allows freemen to own property and the Massachusetts Bay Colony to govern itself, and if the Reverend Mather does not succeed, all will be lost. I do not know what that really means, but it is what the men say at the public meetings.

Then the Widow Holten asked how we wished to be paid for the wool thread. Mem's face lit up with an idea. "Would you happen to have any sturdy shoes you don't need? Liv has holes in her soles."

The Widow looked down at my feet and saw that they are large, while we looked at her feet and saw that they are tiny, and we all laughed. She offered some bayberry tallow, which we were glad of. The Cooper blizzard greatly depleted our store of candles. If only we could see by the light of Mem's eyes when she speaks of *him*, we would not need to make more!

Friday ye 15th

The weather has turned cold again. I never thought I would be grateful for ice, but at this time of year it is better than mud. We are able to walk on the ground without losing our feet.

Susannah's mother sent her here to inquire after our uncle again, for she is still in need of help with some heavy work. Mem elbowed my ribs. She now thinks that Susannah's mother is after our uncle, too! How silly! Mr. Sheldon is barely cold in his grave. I think Mem can only think of one thing now that she is after a husband herself. The two of them sat and talked the morning away, and I don't have to say about which maker of barrels who lives in Haver'il. Thank God they left the venus glass alone.

Saturday ye 16th

Today I was busy knitting and Mem was busy doing nothing when someone came to the door. Mem jumped to get it, and threw the door open without checking the knothole. She denied it later, but I am sure she thought it was Mr. Cooper, for he said to watch for them on Saturdays, but I do not think he meant any Saturday soon. The animals made a fuss. A dust of snow swirled into the room, for the skies had been spitting little dry flakes all the morning, and as the cloud fell away, mine eyes recognized the dark shape that filled the doorway. My throat instantly lumped with dread.

There stood the beggar witch Sarah Goode

with her evil-smelling pipe, and before her stood little Dorcas with purple lips and chattering teeth.

Mem commenced to cough and hack and wave her arms about. Sarah Goode removed her pipe and set it beside the door.

"Please, missies," said Sarah Goode. Her voice was very deep and scratchy, as though her throat were filled with sawdust. "I doth not ask anything for mine self, just a few moments to warm my toes by a fire and a stale scrap of something for mine little daughter to eat."

I swallowed the dread in my throat and made wide eyes at Mem, shaking my head. Uncle Razor Strap would never abide our sharing our miniscule stores with the beggar witch. He could, after all, be home at any moment.

Mem told her the price for apples, and tried to shut the door, but Sarah Goode had her foot in it. "Dorcas is hungry. Ye can see her bones, can't ye?" The beggar pulled back the hood of her daughter's shawl. Dorcas was nothing but skin and bones, with hair like a bird's nest, all stringy and matted around her head.

Mem stepped back. Later she told me she was avoiding the fleas that she could see hopping about, but the woman took it as an invitation.

She pressed Dorcas into the room, and the two of them fell in front of our miserable little fire as if at the feet of the Lord Almighty.

Mem and I looked at each other, and at the backs of the Goodes, and at each other, not knowing what to do. My temples throbbed with nervous fear. We had a witch in our kitchen!

Mem raised her eyebrows mischievously and cleared her throat to speak. "Goody Goode," she said. The name sounded funny, and I stifled a laugh. If she were a gentlewoman she could be called Mistress or Mrs., like Mrs. Parris.

Goody Goode turned her head to listen, but kept her hands over the fire. She looks the part of a hag, with her matted gray hair and creased, leathery face. Yet, she has little Dorcas, and her round middle shows she is carrying another infant, so she cannot be anywhere near as old as she looks.

Mem said, "I hear tell that ye are . . ."

I could not take air, for my fear, and I prayed: Oh, no, dear Lord, do not let Mem ask if Sarah Goode is a witch, and if she does, dear Lord, do not let the witch curse us. We have but one cow and cannot afford to lose our Clover.

"You are . . . married," said my sister.

My breath came back. Mem grinned at me.

She had frightened me on purpose! I did not think it humorous then, but now I smile over my writing of it.

And then how Goody Goode did grumble! Her husband, William, was no good. William had gone bankrupt and lost their property and now had to hire out as a laborer and could not keep a home for his wife and children. William was to blame for all her ills. Her father was no good. Her father had married a shrew and then killed himself, and then the shrew remarried a selfish man who would not give the children their rightful inheritance. Her father was to blame for all her ills. The people of Salem Village were no good. They rebuffed her and accused her of spreading smallpox, and they turned her little child away hungry. The people of Salem Village were to blame for all her ills.

It was time to put on the dinner and bake a pie for the nooning tomorrow. It would be cruel to cook in front of Goody Goode and Dorcas. Even though the Bible says thou shalt not suffer a witch to live, it seemed the only way to get rid of them was to throw them a morsel. Whilst Mem continued to hear about Sarah Goode's sorry life, I went to the root cellar and found two apples that could not be sold for their bruises and worms. Goody Goode devoured every bit, core and all, but Dorcas spit out the unsavory parts onto the floor.

Her mother quickly stooped to pick them up, and whispered something to her daughter, and little Dorcas mumbled something to us that I think was a blessing. On the way out the door the mother mumbled a Psalm under her breath, mixing up some of the words the way the slow-witted children do when learning their catechism. Pray the Lord protect our cow?

January ye 17th
Clover, and all the other animals, seem fine. Mem was wheezing in her sleep, but she often does. I wonder if a witch cursed her in the womb? Off to the Meeting House now.

Later . . .
So much happened today to tell about!

The Reverend Parris preached with great zeal. The Revelation is nigh. All signs point to Doomsday: Indian raids and massacres, epidemics of sickness, and the loss of the charter that allowed us to rule ourselves under the laws of God, until the king took it back seven years ago. Why hath

God turned from His chosen people? Why hath He deemed us unworthy of His rewards? Devout Puritans must search our own hearts — and our actions — for the cause of God's disapproval, before it is too late. We must repent and repair, and tread with care, for the Devil is running amok in Massachusetts.

The morning sermon seemed as infinite as doom itself, though it lasted only three hours, and my mind wandered off the fire and brimstone to plan how I would tell Abigail and Ann about Saturday's visit from the witch. As soon as the final Psalm was sung, I quickly edged my way to follow them.

They were walking with Betty Parris and the Indian slaves who live with the Parrises — Tituba and John Indian, I think they are named. There are not many slaves in Massachusetts. The Parrises used to live in Barbados, and brought their slaves from there.

Clearly this group was heading back to the parsonage for the nooning. I had not been invited, so knew I must capture their interest before they went inside. I called their names. Abigail and Ann halted. The others just glanced at me and moved on into the house.

"God be with you," I said cheerfully.

They did not speak a response, but only sliced me with narrow stares that seemed to cut off my tongue. I could not speak the words I had planned. Frozen, I watched them proceed to the parsonage and go inside. That is when I saw the strangest sight, so strange that I wonder now if the shadows were playing tricks on my eyes.

It looked as if Betty was crouching under a stool with her limbs all twisted! Had she been years younger, I would have thought it a childish game, but Betty is nine years old, and this was the Sabbath!

Back to Ingersoll's Ordinary I went. Many womenfolk were enjoying their victuals and discussing the sermon. Who could be responsible for reaping God's punishment upon us? Had our previous Ministers led us astray? James Bayley? George Burroughs? Deodat Lawson?

All three had left unhappily over the course of the years. In fact, mine uncle claims that the Reverend Samuel Parris must have something wrong with him, for no Minister worth his salt would come to Salem Village after knowing of the quarreling and smiting that drove away the first three. There are those who would have Parris gone by now. That is why they do not pay his salary and stock his woodpile.

"I heard that little man Burroughs was cruel to his two wives," someone offered against him. "And is it true that none of his children was baptized?" "He took a sinful amount of pride in his appearance." "He used to stand on his head and twist his body in all manner of poses." A jumble of voices all made the case against the Reverend Burroughs. Burroughs! What long memories the gossips have. He left the Village eight years ago, back to Maine, where he originally came from. He was Susannah Sheldon's Minister there.

Finally, one of the Church Members rose up, shaking her head, and shook a finger at the rest. Goodwife Martha Corey is the wife of old Giles, who owns a large farm just below the southwestern edge of the Village. Goody Corey puts me in mind of the Widow Ruste because she speaks her mind, and it is a good mind. Goody Corey made the other women know that she would have no part in this sinful gossip. Then she hoisted her little son Thomas up on her hip, turned her back to the women, and said very loudly:

"Who made you?"—*God*. "What else did God make?"—*God made all things*. "Why did God make all things?"—*For His own glory*.

Before long, all the children in the room were piping in to recite their catechism, and so the gossips were silenced. And next comes the best part of the day, but my hand is ready to fall off from writing so much. Besides, Mem is coughing and tossing in bed. I am afraid she will get up and catch me. I shall finish today tomorrow!

Monday, January ye 18th

Abigail and Ann would have relished in the women's skirmish. I was glad they had missed it, and I was not going to tell them what they had missed, either! Mem was off somewhere talking with guess who about guess what. In boredom, I took up a book from Ingersoll's shelf, the Reverend Wigglesworth's *Day of Doom*. Flipping straight to my favorite part, where Christ speaks to the unbaptized infants, I began to read.

> *You sinners are, and such a share*
> *as sinners may expect,*
> *Such you shall have; for I do save*

none by my own elect.
Yet to compare your sin with their
who lived a longer time,
I do confess yours is much less,
though every sin's a crime.

Lost in the book, no longer was I aware of sitting on a hard bench in the cold corner of the inn—until I heard my name, and felt a gentle touch on my shoulder. Goody Corey had sat down next to me, and was listening. I have a habit of moving my lips and whispering when I read, without knowing I am doing it. She apologized for stopping me, but she wanted to speak with me. She told me that I have the voice of an angel!

I am not used to compliments. Praise spoileth the child as surely as molasses rots the teeth. "By the grace of God, Goody Corey," I said, and looked humbly at my hands. I had chewed the nails down to the quick during the sermon. That is another habit I do without realizing.

Goody Corey looked around, seeing if anyone was overhearing us, then bent to tell me privately that her eyes are not what they used to be, and strain to read. Would I be willing to visit her now and then between Sundays and read to her from the Gospel and other texts?

God bless Goody Corey! I cannot contain myself! The Lord hath granted me a regular escape from this prison where I live. It will not be every day, for the wool will not hop upon the spindle and turn itself to thread by magic, but when I have time free, I am to go to the Corey Farm and do my favorite thing on earth!

Oh, I hope her husband will not be there. Giles Corey is rumored to be a brute and a Devilish rogue. Myself, I have not witnessed him lie or cheat or steal, but I have heard his foul mouth in public. He is forever in and out of court with disputes, and was once accused of murdering a farmhand. Apparently the dead man's wife said it was something else that killed him, and the lazy fool deserved the beating, anyhow. Goodman Corey was found innocent. Still, he scares me.

January ye 19th

I just returned from the Corey Farm. It is longer than a mile. By the time I got there, the holes in my shoes had let the wet and the cold into my feet and made me limp into the house. Goody Corey noticed, and immediately went searching for some shoes to fit me. If she had any spares herself, she would give me some. Her own feet are nearly the same size as mine.

Her husband has spares, but his shoes are too big. So are the ones her son outgrew. Besides her own two grown sons, Goody Corey has four stepdaughters and four stepsons-in-law who live on the large properties that belong to Giles. She is a grandmother of children older than her own little Thomas. What a blessing to have a child when most women have become barren. God has surely turned her gray years into golden years!

Upstairs in the eaves, Goody Corey dug through a trunk of old things that belonged to her husband's first wife. She pulled out a pair of stiff old shoes, and they looked decent! But they would not let my feet into them. Finally Goody Corey gave up the search and showed me how to line the bottoms of my shoes with old newspapers soaked in bear grease. It did help keep the wet out.

I will learn much from Goody Corey. She knows the entire Bible by heart! She even knows who beget whom. As I was reading to her, she went about her business in the kitchen, cooking and sewing and tending to Thomas, yet her voice was always there to pick me up whenever I stumbled over a word.

Why did she want me there, when she already knew the Good Book inside her head better than I could read aloud? I asked her, and she said that hearing the Gospel read in the tones of an angel was a pleasure most dear to her. Besides that, she would like to hear *The Narrative of the Captivity and Restoration of Mrs. Mary Rowlandson,* which book she would be next in line to borrow from someone in the Village.

I fairly jumped with joy at hearing that! People often talk about Mrs. Rowlandson's perils and patient sufferings after she was taken in an Indian raid, and her return home to Lancaster after the ransom was paid. It will be a pleasure to read the book she wrote.

Before I left, Goody Corey pulled a bundle of corn from her apron to pay me. I tried to refuse, but she refused to let me! God willing, I will earn enough corn to obtain new soles from the cobbler. However, if Giles Corey ever encounters me at the farm, I am simply to say that I am visiting.

"Keep the corn between ye, me, and thee," she said, and pointed to the fence post.

'Tis a good thing ye can keep secrets, my dear book!

January ye 20th

Today I began reading the narrative of Mrs. Rowlandson. It is as exciting a plot as ever happened to Job or Isaiah, and gives me gooseflesh. It was on February ye 10th, 1675, at the sun rising, when the house of the Reverend Rowlandson and other homes in Lancaster were laid siege. Lancaster is many miles due west from here, but not so far as Connecticut. Many friends and relatives were killed or wounded, but Mrs. Rowlandson and her three children were taken captive. The Indians told her they would not hurt her if she went along with them.

I nodded upon reading of this, for it was something our father used to tell us as part of his frequent lecture about how to behave on the frontier. "If you come upon a wild animal that might eat you, do not run from it, for that will cause it to chase you. Instead, remain calm and sing it away. However, if an animal stalks you with evil intent, and it be an animal that cannot climb, such as a wolf, climb a tree and wait for help. If a bear come clawing at you, it might leave you alone if you roll in a ball on the ground as if dead. And if Indians attack you and do not knock you on the head right away, but take you captive, do whatever they say as quickly as possible, and they will keep you as their own or ransom you back to your family."

Mrs. Rowlandson wrote that she used to think she would rather be killed than taken alive, but when that moment came she chose to go with them rather than end her days. And so she and her children went into captivity. In her book she speaks of several Removes all up and down the wilderness. I can hardly contain myself with suspense to read the next section, but I do not know when I will be able to leave Mem.

She has fallen sick, and this time it is no play-acting to escape work. Her cough has grown painful to hear, and makes a mess in her handkerchief, and she is burning up with fever. I know she must be very ill, for she did not mention Mr. Cooper all day, and what's more she did not eat a thing, though I butchered an old hen that molts more than it lays, so I could make Mem a good healing soup.

I cannot help but worry that Mem has been

cursed by Sarah Goode. Pray Lord keep and protect my sister. If anything were to happen to her, I would like to die myself.

Methinks I shall go check on Clover.

January ye 21st

Last night was Saint Agnes' Eve, which is a traditional time for fortune-telling. I hope Susannah did not waste any eggs.

Oh! Liv, what a fool you have been! Why did I not think of this before? Mem's sickness is no witch's hex! We did feed Sarah Goode and Dorcas, after all, and gave them a warm fire, so what reason would the witch have to afflict Mem? Mem's coughs and chills and fevers must be God's punishment for divining with the venus glass!

I would like to know if Susannah is afflicted, as well. I would walk to the Village to find out, but I cannot leave Mem alone. What has come over me? I do not dare leave her out of my sight. It is as if a hand of iron holds my chest, stopping me from going out the door. I had to force myself out to the barn to tend the animals this morning, and the slop pail needs to be emptied. Even the mighty temptation to read Mrs. Rowlandson's book cannot remove the iron hand from my chest.

I am going to make the bayberry candles now. The work will keep me occupied, and I will feel more at ease knowing we have a good supply. If Mem needs help in the night, there may be need of light in the darkness.

January ye 22nd

Friday already, and Mem still sick abed, sweating with fever though the cold creeps through the walls. If only there were enough logs to heat the house through, perhaps she would recover from what ails her! But such is the way of winter.

Even in the Corey kitchen, the fire's heat cannot reach far from the hearth. The invisible cold seeps into bones as stubbornly as it creeps through the walls, even though pains have been taken to fill every crack. No mouse, no bat, no speck of light can creep through the chinked walls at the Corey Farm, yet the bitter air succeeds.

If cold air can creep through strong wood, it is no wonder that evil spirits make way into the weak hearts of men. The world is full of perils, seen and unseen.

Today the Sheldons came to call, Susannah and her mother, too. Susannah looked in fine health. Why, God, does Mem receive punishment while

Susannah does not? Forgive me, God; I should not have written that. Like Mrs. Rowlandson, I must trust in Thy wisdom and design.

The minute they got inside, Susannah set to whispering with Mem, while the mother looked about the place suspiciously, poking her nose around the doorway to the bedroom and craning her neck to see up into the loft. The chickens had not settled down quite yet, and were making noise. It sounded as if someone might be moving around upstairs. Susannah's mother then said, very loudly, even though I was two feet away from her mouth, "Girls, if your uncle does not wish to do work for me, I wish he would have the common decency to tell me so himself, instead of sending messages back and forth between children."

Later, Mem and I laughed over it. At least the Widow Sheldon does not know that our uncle is gone from this place. Instead, she suspects that he has been avoiding her.

The Widow Holten, on the other hand, is starting to wonder. She came by today, as well, to bring us more wool to spin, which someone gave her in trade. She said, "Girls, I have not seen your uncle about the Village in some time, not even at Ingersoll's." It is true that our uncle enjoys the company and the rum at Ingersoll's Ordinary.

"Really?" I said, trying to sound surprised.

"Why has he changed his habits so?" the Widow Holten asked. "It is not good to be reclusive. Is there something the matter? Can I be of help?"

At that moment Mem came coughing from the bedroom, her skin pale except for her flushed cheeks.

"My dear!" said the Widow. "You are some ill. Have you taken any asafetida in wine?" And so the Widow was distracted from sticking her nose in our uncle's whereabouts.

This cat-and-mouse game of telling the truth without being honest is not fun anymore. God, I beg You, please send our uncle home before one of our Widows comes back?

January ye 23rd

The news has got around that Mem has got something ailing her. Several people of the neighborhood turned out to see her today. In fact, our little house was so crammed with visitors come to pray for Mem's health that it felt almost like a Sunday Meeting instead of a Saturday afternoon. With each new knock at the door, Mem looked hopefully to see the face behind it, but Mr. Cooper did not come. I think that is a blessing. Her coughing and hacking are not very attractive.

The Widow Holten brought her medicinal vapors to drink in a tea. The Sheldons brought some honey cakes. Someone else brought a pomander of sweet-smelling herbs. Mem sat still on her carding stool, her hands crossed demurely on her lap except when she was lifting her handkerchief to her mouth, and listened patiently to the advice and prayers for her health. From the way her hem was twitching, though, I think she must have been fluttering her toes like hummingbird wings, wanting to fly back to bed.

After a time the room fell silent, and the visitors all gazed at her expectantly, as if waiting for something to happen. They stirred with interest when she excused herself to go outside. Those nearest the door followed her partway to the privy, in fact. Those remaining inside cocked their ears to better hear her empty her lungs.

When she returned to her stool, the visitors watched with intent interest as she folded her handkerchief to a clean spot. The faces of the crowd sagged with disappointment. This struck me as very strange, until finally a small child piped up, "When is she going to scream blasphemies?"

This broke Mem's demure posture. "What did he say?" she asked, mighty irritated. Maybe Mr. Cooper should have come. Mem looks pretty when her cheeks turn red.

As the mother hushed the child, my mind reeled. "I do not understand," I said. Mem may jest about silly things. She may even do foolish things such as use a venus glass in secret. However, she would not speak with disrespect for the Lord! Where did the neighbors come up with that idea!

There was a murmuring in the gathering, and someone said, "Is Remembrance not afflicted like little Betty and Abigail? That is what I heard."

Afflicted? What ill had befallen the girls? I was sore confused.

"You had better explain yourselves," Mem said.

Then it came out that the Reverend's daughter and niece have been contorting their bodies into unnatural positions and uttering terrible sounds that mostly make no sense, though sometimes blasphemies are heard. The deacons and midwives of the neighborhood have rushed to their aid. Word has gotten out that Mem is afflicted with violent illness, and so our friends and neighbors also came running to her aid. (Methinks they ran to the parsonage first but could not find room to stand.)

"There is no sport here," whined the child. "Can we go home now?" The child's mother yanked him close to her by the arm and covered his mouth, but it did not take long for the kitchen to clear.

After the dust settled I sat quietly trying to sort my scrambled thoughts. The image of Betty under the chair last Sunday floated up. How long had she been behaving so strangely? And when had Abigail begun? What could have caused such horror in the house of a Minister? This did not sound like any common sickness I had ever seen or heard tell about. Had the Devil gotten into the girls?

At that thought, a sense of doom pressed down on me. It felt as heavy as the stench of the sickroom where my father and brothers lay dying, one after the other. Something terrible is going to happen in Salem Village. I can feel it in my bones, as surely as the caterpillar can feel a long winter coming.

January ye 24th

Mem is too sick to attend the Sabbath today. Even if she could walk and breathe at the same time and get herself to the Meeting House, the congregation would not appreciate her noise. The clattering of feet trying to stay warm in the unheated building is enough for the ears to contend with. I told her I will stay home with her, but she insisted that I go and bring back news of the affliction. So I will push my way past the iron hand that stops me at the door and go to the Meeting House. At least the weather is dry; I will enjoy the fresh air.

January ye 25th

The affliction was all anyone could speak about when the Reverend Parris wasn't preaching. Methinks more of the faithful were watching Betty and Abigail out of the corners of their eyes than were paying attention to the sermon. The two girls did nothing out of the ordinary, however, except yawn frequently behind their hands. All of that twisting and screaming must be exhausting.

That vile Hobbs girl tried to get with me and tell me again about her fun in the Maine woods with the Devil. I told her mine ears did not want to hear her nonsense and went to sit with Goody Corey at the nooning. She informed me that Mrs. Mary Rowlandson misses me! I told her that I also miss Mrs. Rowlandson. I am eager to continue reading as soon as Mem recovers from her fever.

It is Monday. It is snowing deep again. Mem

hopes the white sky is a sign that the Coopers will stop today.

January ye 26th

The Coopers did not come, but that is the least of my worries. Most of the chickens have stopped laying! Over the past weeks they have slowed in production. Some slowing is normal during the cold, dark winter, but we keep them indoors so they will not stop. Maybe they are scared of Mem's coughing. Chickens do not like to be scared. I hope that is the reason, and not a witch. If Sarah Goode has cursed them, we might as well put them in the stew pot.

January ye 27th

Susannah came for eggs. I was able to give her two, enough to make her cake rise. She brought terrible news from a messenger riding through on the way to Boston yesterday. The Maine settlement of York was attacked on Saturday. Those Devilish French and Wabanakis! My first fear was for our brother, Benjamin, but it turned out that no militia was present at the time. He was safe from guns and hatchets if not from smallpox and scurvy.

Fifty English residents died, and one hundred

were taken prisoner. Before the raiders marched away they did let the young children and old women go, praise God. The buildings for five miles around were burnt, the livestock slaughtered. The militia arrived from New Hampshire too late to do anything but look at the ashes.

I am so glad we do not live on the frontier anymore, and have to live with the fear of every crackling twig, every sudden shadow. Yet, if it would mean that Mem and I could live again with our father and brothers, and our stepmother, I would not hesitate to go back.

Later . . .

The Widow Holten came and brought Mem some tinctures for her cough. She also brought news from Boston. The king has appointed our new Royal Governor, Sir William Phips, who was Maine-born and made his own fortune. There are those who dislike him. Still, all agree that it is good that he be our leader rather than a stranger the king sends over on a ship. Perhaps there is hope yet that the king will reinstate the charter allowing the Massachusetts Bay Colony to keep charge of itself.

The Widow Holten looked suspiciously around

the house again. She said in a loud voice that she has given up on having our uncle help her with *anything*.

January ye 28th

It is our turn to have Lecture Day in the Village today. I do not like to leave Mem, but I do not like to miss a sermon. Lecture Day is a time to see different folk who come from towns all around, and the Ministers always give their best speeches. So I will go.

January ye 29th

Poor Mem. Here she be lying in bed coughing up her lungs, while I be in church singing with the Coopers! They had heard about Lecture Day in the Village. They planned their homeward travel so they could stop at the Meeting House with eager hopes of meeting our uncle.

Upon first sight of Darcy limping toward me I noticed his misshapen leg with surprise. I had forgot to picture it in my memories of him.

I thought quickly about what to say about mine uncle, and I stammered in my wording. "He . . . has . . . so much to do, he . . . did not have time to sit still today."

Mr. Cooper nodded as if he understood, and Darcy hid a smile. Methinks they thought I was trying to cover up for our uncle avoiding the sermon, and they were amused by it. Then they looked about with bright faces, searching for Mem. They dropped their smiles when I told them she was home sick in bed. If our uncle were home to chaperone, they said they would come by and give her well wishes and prayers in person.

Is Mem right about her Mr. Cooper? Does he intend to court her? Oh, I hope so, because now that she has heard of his visit, she has set her heart on him.

Before the lecture, people stood about describing and debating the affliction of Betty and Abigail. One fellow reported that he saw Betty drop to the floor and cross her limbs in several unnatural ways and cry out nonsense with her eyes wide but unseeing. It seemed she was in a trance. Another reported that Abigail came running toward him with her arms outstretched like an eagle, crying, "Whisht! Whisht! Whisht!" Then she grabbed a burning log from the fire and tossed it across the room! Tituba Indian, the slave, raced after her, fixing the damage.

"Nothing afflicts these girls that a good thrashing will not cure," said one man. "They are making mischief to escape their work and gain attention."

I do not know. It sounds to me as if some spirit with a will of its own rides them.

Saturday ye 30th of January

Goody Corey lost patience with waiting for me to come reading, so she brought the book to me! She came with two of her stepdaughters and their yarn. Little Thomas brought his wooden building blocks to play with on the floor with the dog and cat. Mem sat with us for a few minutes but could not stay warm; her fever turned to chills when she got up. Goody Corey implored her to get back in bed. We sat all around her there, and Goody Corey led earnest prayers for about an hour. Then the three women set to knitting while I read.

In her book, Mrs. Rowlandson told of the barbarous Wabanakis and how they roared and sang and danced around a fire celebrating the day. They were glad to have made her and the other English so unhappy. The one daughter she had with her was in a pitiful state, badly injured, and running a fever from the wound. The other two children were separated from her. She wrote that the picture around her was "a lively resemblance of hell."

"I do not understand why God allows the heathens to survive," Mem said bitterly. "The Indians are evil Devils!" She is passionate about it because she deeply resents the raid on our homestead.

Goody Corey stopped knitting and looked up into the corner of the ceiling. The usual rustling of the chickens in the loft above seemed loud, though I usually do not notice them at all. Then Goody sighed deeply and said to Mem that we cannot know God's plan, but we can know the hearts of men, and the Indians are only men, not Devils.

Mem gasped at this, and I was shocked as well, but I leaned forward to hear more as Goody Corey described her thoughts. She said the Indians behave badly because they are angry. All men become angry when they have been insulted. They do not like that the Englishmen have come and taken control of their lands, on which their ancestors roamed freely for generations.

"But the Indians sold the land," Mem insisted. "It is ours to do with as we please. They cannot take it back again!"

Goody Corey nodded and thought again and

then spoke. She used to think the same way, she said, until she got to know a Wampanoag woman who married a whaler and became a Christian years ago in Salem Town. Indians do not have the same idea of land that Englishmen do, the woman told Goody Corey. Englishmen divide it into parcels, each his own, and nobody else has rights to use it except for sale or rent. The Indians share the land. They all live together on it. And so when they sold the land, they thought they were giving the Englishmen the right to share it. The woman told Goody Corey that the Indians did not expect to be driven off their lands, and lose their rights to it, and even be killed over it. That is why they are angry.

And the French are not helping matters any. They, Goody Corey said, are the real Devils. Unlike the Indians, they know about God and Jesus and the Bible and still, they spur the natives on in their warring.

I tried, but I did not understand what she was saying. I thought Goody Corey was a Gospel woman. How could she hold sympathy with Godless barbarians who slaughter innocent Puritans in their homes?

One of the stepdaughters complained that

Goody Corey had distracted her and made her drop a stitch and now she had to unravel five rows of knitting. Then the other one said Goody Corey was too opinionated about things she could not possibly know, and should leave the thinking to the men. Goody Corey laughed at them and shook her head as if they were the ones speaking strangeness. We then talked about the coloring of yarn and how to make a red dye that will not bleed in the rain.

I have decided I do not know what to think of Goody Corey!

Monday ye 1st of February

Yesterday I pushed past the iron hand again and trod alone to Sunday Meeting, worrying over Mem with every step. Just when she seems better in one part she gets worse in some other part. For instance, her fever seems to have broken — but so has one of her ribs, from the violent coughing. So now every time she coughs or sneezes, she also howls with the pain that stabs her like a toothache. If only we could tie a string to her rib and yank it out to relieve her suffering as my father used to remove the teeth that tortured him.

What could Mem have done to provoke such

punishment from God? It could not be the venus glass, or surely Susannah would also be sick. Has Mem committed a grievous sin that I do not know about?

The affliction in the parsonage continues. Some people cannot stop their mouths moving about it long enough to swallow their bread. There are some among the adults who say the antics of the girls are nothing but idle sport to entertain themselves and get out of work. If we ignore them, the affliction will go away. Some say that God is moving in Betty and Abigail, and bringing them Christlike visions, as would be befitting the house of a Minister. And some say the opposite: that the Devil hath gotten into them, to interfere with God's work.

Goody Corey told me she wonders if the Reverend Parris is too harsh on the girls, and has made them crazy. I think her theory is crazy, and I pray she does not say it in public!

Before the sermon I tried to speak with Abigail Williams and inquire as to her health, but she ignored me as if I were as invisible as air, and went to find Ann Putnam. The two of them spent the nooning together in a world of two. Abigail looks hale and hearty, as if nothing in the world ails her, but Betty looks pale and frail. She stayed close by her mother with her eyes closed, even throughout the sermon.

If she were not the daughter of the Minister himself, the Tithing Man would have come around with his staff to open her eyes. His staff has a soft hare's foot dangling off one end for the women and girls, and a heavy knob on the other end for the men and boys. I have never fallen asleep in church before, but Mem has awakened more than once to the tickle of the hare's foot in the face. The Tithing Man mostly keeps people from sleeping, but boys will also be rapped pitilessly if they are too wide awake.

One time a man from Lynn, who was snoring through the sermon, got rapped on the noggin. The sleepy fellow was so bewildered that he jumped up and struck the Tithing Man back before realizing that he was not home in bed. He was sore ashamed and was publicly whipped as a warning. I doubt he ever napped at Meeting again.

Mine uncle says that if he ever joins the church, he should like to be a Tithing Man. He would think it great sport to see that everyone remains attentive in Meeting except himself. However, our uncle would not like watching over ten families for the rest of the week.

Besides collecting donations for the church, the Tithing Man must make sure that the children he is assigned to learn their catechism. He must keep boys from swimming in water, and watch the ordinaries to make sure nobody drinks too heavily or engages in idle games. The Tithing Man also keeps a close eye on all the bachelors to make sure they respect the virtue of other men's wives and daughters.

Actually, the last duty is too big for the Tithing Man alone. Everyone keeps a close eye on the bachelors.

At the nooning both of the Widows found me to ask after our uncle. The Widow Holten said she had not seen him in church since the leaves fell. She worries over his soul, which must be hungry for the nourishment of God's word. I thanked her for her thoughtfulness.

The Widow Sheldon said that she had not seen him in town since the leaves fell. She worried over his spirits, which must be low to keep him out of the company of others. I thanked her, as well, though I do not feel very grateful. Now I pray that our uncle will COME HOME SOON, before those two put their heads together and decide to chase the truth.

Tuesday ye 16th of February

I could not write for these two weeks because I ran out of ink! It has taken me this long to make new. First I had to wait for the snow to melt, so I could find walnut shells and pheasant feathers in the woods. Then I had to wait for Mem to mend, so she would leave the house. I did not want her to see me making ink or she would wonder why I needed it.

She is feeling better now, and went to Sunday Meeting. Yesterday I made the ink when she went to the Village to trade some apples for some things she needed to cook in case the Coopers came (which they did not). Now I am free to write, because she has gone to Susannah Sheldon's with her sewing and gossip.

I found ten walnut shells and wrapped them in a cloth, then crushed them with a hammer. The shells went in a pan with some water and simmered until the liquid turned dark brown and much of the water boiled away. The ink came off the fire to cool. Then I strained it into the inkpot and added vinegar and salt to preserve it. Out came the knife and off came the end of a feather on an angle. Filled with ink, my pen was made and hid away.

When Mem got home she sniffed the air and asked me what I had been burning this time.

Oh, how I love to write! Words flowing out my hand onto the page feel much the same as singing. A calm descends upon me, even when I am angry. I have been angry a great deal of late, and had no place to put it except prayer, and I think God is probably very glad I have ink again. He is probably tired of hearing me complain.

Wednesday ye 17th

Here are some things that have made me angry:

The chickens have laid no eggs at all. I told Goody Corey about them when she brought Mrs. Rowlandson to visit again. Mem said she was sure Sarah Goode has cursed them, and I agreed. Goody Corey smiled at us as if she were wise and we were silly children. Then she asked if the chickens had been kept calm, warm, dry, fed, and especially watered. She said chickens need a constant source of fresh water or they will dry up.

Hearing this, I recalled the stubborn match I had lost against Mem the day we had no water. Hot shame rushed through me and made me shrink inside. Perhaps it was my own fault the chickens were not laying, and so I was angry with myself.

I was angry with mine uncle. I am still angry with mine uncle. Need I say why? No, but I shall say it, anyhow. Last time Goody Corey came with her knitting, she kept testing the air with her nose like a rabbit does, until Mem offered her a handkerchief. Goody Corey said she was sniffing because the place smells entirely like girls, and not a bit like a man.

Mem thought very quickly to make a joke about how Goody Corey should come back after Uncle has used the chamber pot, and then she will smell him. Then Goody Corey's stepdaughters laughed and told stories about their husbands, and we were off the topic of Uncle Invisible. Still, it was a narrow escape. I cannot imagine how we are going to keep his secret for very long with a wise nose like Goody Corey's attempting to sniff him out.

I was also angry with Mem. There she lay abed for week upon week, leaving all the work to me, and keeping me home because I was afraid to leave her alone when I could have been at Goody Corey's reading. If Mem were not sick, Goody Corey would not have stuck her nose into our manless house in the first place. Mem could not help it, yet I could not help feeling angry with her.

Staring at her face one afternoon while she was sleeping, I saw my father in it. Why did he have to go and make a homestead on the frontier when he could have stayed in Hartford doing a trade and watching over his family? He wanted his own land and instead he lost his life. And so I was angry with my father.

Reading Mrs. Rowlandson's book causes me to remember my stepmother. I could never be angry with her, for she sacrificed herself to save me and Mem and Benjamin. However, I am very angry with the Indians who took her captive. It makes me angry to read of Mrs. Rowlandson's travails in the wilderness. She had to watch her little daughter die after nine miserable days of moaning in pain from the wounds she received in the attack. The captives were forced to go for days without food and water. Our chickens lead a better life, even if they lay no eggs.

Goody Corey makes me very angry. I do not understand how she can have any compassion for people who rejoice at killing Englishmen and taking their scalps, but she does. Each time we read about the Removes of Mrs. Rowlandson from one camp to the next, she will say something to defend the Indians.

For instance, on the Third Remove an Indian came back from a raid with a basket of plunder and brought a Bible to Mrs. Rowlandson. The Indians allowed her to keep it and read it. Goody Corey said this means that not all Indians are doing the work of the Devil, and some of them may even be doing the work of the Lord. We protested this, but she reminded us that God's will controls all events, even the awful ones. She is right about that much. Though it be painful to accept, the Indians can only do what God allows them to do.

Goody Corey recommends that rather than being blinded by our fear and hatred, we should be focusing our eyes to study what God is showing us. Perhaps God allows the Indians to burn our homesteads and take our scalps and captives because He does not desire Puritans to own the frontier. Perhaps He wishes the wilderness to remain with the Indians for some reason beyond our understanding.

How does Goody Corey come up with these strange ideas? Her husband's daughters say she is going through the change of life and losing her senses.

But most of all I was angry that I had no ink. Now I am happy.

Thursday ye 18th

Though she makes me angry, I am eager to go to Goody Corey's and read the Sixth Remove of Mrs. Rowlandson. During the Fifth Remove, the English army was following the Indians that held Mrs. Rowlandson. The army stopped at a river, though the Indians crossed it ahead of them. Why is it that an army of men could not keep up with squaws and children traveling bag and baggage?!

Mrs. Rowlandson suggested that God did not find a way for the English to pass the river because we are "not ready for so great a mercy as victory and deliverance." Goody Corey nodded in that way of hers, and my head spun.

I hope the English will be brave enough to get their feet wet today, but I doubt they will, as the book is not half done.

Friday ye 19th

The Indians burned their wigwams and moved on quickly this time. We read the Seventh Remove and part of the Eighth, as well. I read with tears in my voice as I imagined Mrs. Rowlandson fighting with others for food. She found two ears of corn, but had one stolen from her when she turned her back. An Indian gave her some horse liver, which she laid to roast on the coals, and half of it was snatched away from her before it cooked, and so she was forced to eat it raw, yet she was so hungry that it tasted savory.

On the Eighth Remove, she got to see her son. What a joyful passage that was! They read together from the Bible before they parted, and took strength in His wonderful power to save them from death in the hands of their enemies. But then Mrs. Rowlandson had to travel with her master to see King Philip, who was leader of the Indians.

She described being alone in the midst of a great crowd of pagans, and listening to the Indians rejoicing over their gains and victories. Her brave heart failed, and she fell to weeping in front of the crowd of pagans. Goody Corey and her husband's daughters and I wept with her, and read no more that day.

Saturday ye 20th

The weather has warmed enough that I can take my pen out of the house without the ink freezing. Now I sit in the hayloft of the barn, with the sun shining in on me. It will be a pleasure to write anytime the mood strikes, as opposed to waiting until Mem is out and about or in a deep sleep. My journal and pen ride flat in one of my pockets. They can travel with me wherever I go, and need not always hide in the root cellar.

Mem is certain that the Coopers will come to call today. Perhaps they will. It has been three weeks since they attended Lecture Day in the Village. However, we still have not seen hide nor hair of our uncle. Even if they do come knocking, Mem will not receive any courting without a snowstorm to chaperone.

As for myself, I look forward to seeing Darcy, but not as much as I look forward to finding out what happens next to Mrs. Rowlandson. While Mem was cooking and cleaning, I went back to the Corey Farm to finish the Eighth Remove.

After her weeping the pagans took pity on Mrs. Rowlandson. They promised they would not hurt her, and gave her two spoonfuls of meal and half a pint of peas to comfort her. Then she went to see King Philip.

He asked her to smoke with him, which is taken as a great compliment among the Indians. However, Mrs. Rowlandson will not touch tobacco. She calls it "a bait the Devil lays to make men lose their precious time." I think she is right. Our uncle likes his pipe and when he smokes it he does not do anything else.

King Philip asked Mrs. Rowlandson to make a shirt for his son, and she did and was paid a shilling. She offered the money to her master, but he let her keep it and she bought something to eat.

I was surprised to hear of these kindnesses from the cruel savages. Goody Corey did not seem surprised at all. She said that it is only natural that the Indians would treat Mrs. Rowlandson more kindly as they come to know her better. Now they see her as a fellow creature who eats and weeps and has talents to share, the same as they do.

Her stepdaughter scoffed at this and said King Philip is only treating Mrs. Rowlandson well because none of the Indians can make good English shirts. Her master let her keep the money because he was afraid to take away what the king gave. Besides, he must realize that Mrs.

Rowlandson needs to get enough to eat if he is to ransom her back to her husband for a good price. If she can buy her own food, he does not need to feed her.

Methinks the stepdaughter makes better sense than Goody Corey.

During her time in this place, Mrs. Rowlandson was paid to make other items for the Indians. King Philip invited her to dinner. She also saw her son and several other English prisoners. We leave her with news that some Indians have brought back some horses from a raid. She wishes they would ride her to Albany to ransom her, but she holds little hope that they will do so. We shall find out next week.

Outside, I hear the feet of many horses and the wheels of a big wagon coming. The Coopers!

Later . . .

The Coopers seemed mighty exasperated to find that our uncle was not at home *again*. We told them the truth: that when our uncle went off on this current errand, he took a bag with him. We suspected he would be gone the night, at least.

Mem invited them to come in and have dinner with us, anyhow. They looked at each other and spoke with their eyes. I could not understand what they meant.

Finally Mr. Cooper cleared his throat and said that there was a matter of some urgency that he must discuss with our uncle. Would we kindly give him a message? We of course agreed, Mem most eagerly. Did he know why?

We found Mr. Cooper paper and pen, and he wrote our uncle a letter.

Dear Mr. Trembley,

As you know, my son and I greatly appreciated the generosity of your household during the terrible blizzard of last month. I would like to thank you in person, and also discuss with you a matter of some major importance. I request an audience with you at your earliest convenience. You are cordially invited to visit my household in Haver'il, or I shall be glad to return to your home on another day if you kindly let me know when you will be available. I will look forward to receiving a message from you soon.

> *Sincerely,*
> *Jones Darcy Cooper, Senior*

What are we going to do? It matters not to Mem that we have no uncle to show the note. Her heart has turned into a giant goose-down pillow. She floats about the house on the tips of her toes, as if in a trance. She is convinced Mr. Cooper intends to ask for her hand in marriage. I hope for her heart's sake that Mr. Cooper has no other business in mind — and that our uncle gets himself home soon to make a reply.

Monday ye 22nd

The affliction, the affliction, the affliction. It is all anyone would talk about at the Meeting House yesterday. Last week was the same, though I had no ink to write about it.

Now the debate has turned from "what is the matter" to "what shall be done about it," for Dr. Griggs has made a diagnosis. The Reverend Parris has been taking Betty and Abigail to various physicians, of course, to identify their ailments. They have treated the affliction with parsnip seeds, asafetida in wine, spirits of castor with oil of amber, and all the other usual remedies. The only one they have not tried is the one Goody Corey recommends: Ignore it and it will go away.

They have tried fasting and prayer, the strongest

cure of all—yet the strange fits continue. And so Dr. Griggs, finding no physical cause, has finally pronounced that the Evil Hand is on them.

Most Villagers agree that the Devil is somehow causing the fits. However, he cannot do so without the help of a witch. Who can it be? That is what everyone wants to know now, but the girls do not know whom to blame.

Some of the Villagers say it must be Sarah Goode. She was seen begging at the parsonage recently, and she went away muttering. However, the girls had fallen sick weeks before that. Others say it is probably Tituba Indian, who obviously was not baptized as an infant or raised Christian. Many additional names have been suggested, mostly folks who fail to attend church regularly. I listened with my heart galloping in my chest, dreading to hear mine uncle's name. Thank God nobody thought to mention him.

The longer the affliction goes on, the deeper my fear sinks into me. Whether Satan is riding these girls, or the Lord is working within them to drive the Devil out, or they are making their odd postures and ridiculous speeches on their own free will for some reason, I do not know. But it is clear that the people of Salem Village will not rest until the girls have returned to normal. The people will pinch and squeeze at the matter till it bursts like a pustule.

Tuesday ye 23rd of February

No ride to Albany for Mrs. Rowlandson. Her troubles and blessings continue. She has met a squaw who gives her food, and invites her back, and would buy her if able. Mrs. Rowlandson seems surprised that strangers would be so kind. (Of course this came as no surprise to Goody Corey.)

Happiness never to last long in this life, in the Tenth Remove we find that another Indian hunts her down, and makes her leave the kind squaw's wigwam, and kicks her all along until she goes home, where nobody will give her any of the venison they are roasting.

The Eleventh Remove goes quickly with nothing happening, except Mrs. Rowlandson is dizzy. I hope she is not sick. We shall find out in the Twelfth Remove. I hope I can get me to the Corey Farm tomorrow. Outside, the rain is driven to soak the ground. My feet dread to tread.

My bag of reading corn grows larger. It hides in the root cellar with my book. I do not wish Mem to cook up my shoes or feed them to the chickens.

She knows I read to Goody Corey, and asks me each day what has become of Mrs. Rowlandson, but I have not told her about the corn. It is between me, Goody Corey, and the fence post.

Wednesday ye 24th

The rain paused for a time, and the Widow Holten came today for her thread. She gave us some money, and a piece of bear meat. Mem boiled the meat with ground nuts the way Mrs. Rowlandson describes as most savory. It does not taste anything like chicken. It made me want to spit! Methinks Mrs. Rowlandson has been hungry too long and lost her taste.

As for the Widow, she did not say a word about our uncle, but studied the household closely inside and out. Through the knothole I watched her leave. She surveyed the yard all up and down, and looked a long time at the log pile, with its split firewood all stacked neatly between two pines, whose boughs make a roof against the elements. Darcy chopped more for us on Saturday while his father composed the letter.

Instead of going straight to the gate, she followed the path to the barn, placing her feet very carefully, like a deer picking its way through the woods. Had she lost her head? Later, when I went out to tend the animals, I studied the path and realized what she had been doing: putting her feet in the shoe prints. Some have frozen into the mud, and some have crusted into the patches of snow. Most of the prints belong to me, but some are Mem's little cat feet, and the Coopers left some footprints behind them on Saturday. The Widow Holten was looking to see if our uncle has set foot around here.

Praise God for sinking the Cooper men's feet in our snow!

Thursday ye 25th of February

Found a spot of clear sky to escape me to the Corey Farm. Mrs. Rowlandson is not sick, I was relieved to find. Not exactly. On the Twelfth Remove she had to carry a heavy load, which hurt her back. The Indians are all in a cantankerous mood, treating her meanly. She complained about the skin off her back, and one told her it would be no matter if her head came off, too!

Susannah came while I was gone at Goody Corey's. We had no eggs to give her, but she had gossip to give us. The Parrises are attending Lecture Day out of town, and Mary Sibley has given directions to their slaves to make a witch cake while they are gone. Mix rye meal with urine from the bewitched, bake the cake in the ashes, and then give it to the dog to eat. This is supposed to hurt the witch, and cause her to reveal herself.

I am surprised that Mary Sibley decided to take matters into her own hands. Everyone knows that Mr. Parris would never approve of fighting magic with magic. I doubt that anyone will dare tell him, in fact. The whole Village will know what happened in his house today except him!

Mary Sibley lives near the parsonage and has often gone to help the girls. She means well, and only wishes to relieve Abigail and Betty of their torment. If there truly is a witch at work, I hope the witch cake gets her off their backs and we can all be done with it.

Friday ye 26th of February

Mem went to town early in the morning with a basket of apples to trade, despite the soaking rain driven by the east wind. That is how keenly she wanted to find out what happened after the dog ate the witch cake.

All hell has broken loose! When Mr. and Mrs. Parris returned from Lecture, their girls were suffering worse than ever. What's more, Abigail's and Betty's eyes have been opened to the Invisible World. Now they can see what torments them: the figures of actual people come to pinch and hit them!

It is not just one witch, but witches!

And that is not all. The affliction has spread! Ann Putnam is now suffering, and so is Elizabeth Hubbard. The witches must know to hurt Ann because she is Abigail's friend, and I imagine they are hurting Elizabeth to get back at her uncle, Dr. Griggs, for diagnosing the Evil Hand.

My hand is a Shaky Hand. There is no warm blood running through my veins, only cold fear. I can barely move. Mem, however, is filled with excitement, and has gone back to spend the afternoon at Ingersoll's Ordinary, where she will not miss a thing.

Later . . .

The girls have blamed Tituba for their pain. Even though she herself is in another room, her invisible specter comes and pushes them around. Her specter tries to choke them, and twists their arms and backs in ways beyond their natural ability. Mr. Parris demands to know who else torments them, but they cannot yet tell who it be.

There are many visitors at the parsonage. Ministers have come from around the area to see the affliction for themselves, and pray it out of the girls. The Reverend John Hale of Beverly is there, and the Reverend Noyes of Salem, and others. They have talked to Tituba, and she has told them that she made a witch cake! But she did not mention Mary Sibley. She also said that her mistress in her own country was a witch, and taught her some countermagic. Tituba declared that she herself was not a witch, though.

The Ministers agree that the hand of Satan is in the girls, but they do not believe the Devil needs witches to do his dirty work. It may be true, then, that Tituba is not a witch. They do not recommend any further use of countermagic, and they do not recommend that Tituba be arrested and put on trial to discover her guilt. They recommend that the Parrises sit still and wait upon the Providence of God to see what time might discover.

The Parrises may sit still, but will the Villagers?

Saturday ye 27th

Goody Corey's to read, or Ingersoll's to hear the news? Both beckoned me. Mem, of course, rushed herself to the Village at first opportunity. I greased my paper soles and headed for the Corey Farm.

In the Thirteenth Remove an Indian tells Mrs. Rowlandson that her son's master roasted her son, and he was very good meat. We are hoping that the brute is lying, because Indians think it is fun to scare people like that, when in rushes Goody Corey's husband all breathless with news.

Ann Putnam has identified the apparition that has been tormenting her since Thursday, and nagging her to sign the Devil's Book. It is Sarah Goode!

Nobody was surprised to hear that. Goody Corey said she was wondering when Sarah Goode would be named. In a sarcastic voice she said it was very wise of the Devil to entrust his book to someone who cannot read or write. Goodman Corey told his wife she was the one being *wise,* and it was not very *smart.* She said he was being *stupid* to get caught up in this witch hunt based on the antics of little girls with wild imaginations. And on it went.

Whenever they are together, they argue. It amazes me that Goody Corey dares disagree with her husband! She does not do it in public, though.

After a while Giles Corey went back to the

Village with two of his sons-in-law "to help," they said. Apparently it takes the strength of men to hold the girls in place so they do not hurt themselves flailing around or twisting themselves into supernatural knots.

Mrs. Rowlandson is telling us of meeting an Englishman who has just been taken prisoner and bears news of Mr. Rowlandson. He is well, thank God, but melancholy, of course. Well, in comes Goodman Corey again with fresh news. On her way back from an errand to the Putnams, Elizabeth Hubbard was stalked by a wolf that Sarah Goode sent after her! Not only that, but she has been harassed by the spirit of Goody Osborn. I have never seen Osborn, though I think I once heard she was involved with a legal squabble with the Putnams over land.

Goody Corey made a scoffing noise and said she could not believe her ears. Sarah Osborn is so sickly and frail, she has not even been to Sunday Meeting in a long time. How could a bedridden woman do the Devil's hard work?

Goodman Corey said he believes Osborn be a witch because she lived in the same house with her second husband before they were married.

Goody Corey gasped and turned very red very

fast, and asked since when does being a sinner make one a witch?

My heart dropped to my throat as I remembered that Goody Corey's son Ben is mulatto, and was born to her when she was married to her first husband, Goodman Rich. She and her son lived in Salem Town separately from her husband for ten years until he died. Then she married Giles Corey. I do not know what happened to give her a mulatto son, but I do know that the circumstances did not prevent her from becoming a full Church Member, and taking the sacraments. She is a good Gospel woman and among God's elect now. But I am sure Goody Corey felt insulted by her husband's words about Sarah Osborn.

After she turned red, she called him an old fool, and sent me home. Methinks she was just getting started and did not want me to hear the rest.

February ye 28th, the Sabbath

Darcy Cooper came to Meeting today, but without his father! We thought that strange at first, but then he managed to stammer to Mem that his father had not heard from our uncle. Darcy had come to receive his answer to Mr. Cooper's message. His trembling voice held enough emotion for both himself and his father.

Mem and I looked at each other with wide eyes. How could we have forgotten to do something about that letter? As much as Mem was preoccupied with the courting of Mr. Cooper, she has become distracted by the discovery of the witches.

Mem told Darcy that we deeply regret our uncle's failure to respond, just as we regret that he is not a regular churchgoer. Would Darcy like to come by after the service and speak with our uncle, though? We certainly have every hope that he will be home. (And that is the truth!) Darcy blushed at the invitation and nodded his acceptance to his shoes.

Darcy's leg is not so crooked, as I recall, nor his face so ugly. His voice is even more beautiful when he lifts it in song. I could hear him above all the others on the men's side of the church, for even though he did not sing loudly, he sang lovely, and the men around him followed his lead. Normally there is much squeaking above and grumbling below the key of our tortured tunes, with some singing to York melody and others to St. David's and running over to Oxford by the end.

As we broke for the nooning, Goody Corey

looked around and asked who the songbird might be. There were many new faces in the crowd today, driven through the rain by the excitement of the witch affliction. I introduced Darcy, and asked him to sing Goody Corey's favorite Psalm, but all he could do was blush and mumble. He is as humble as a dandelion. He will make some girl a kind husband someday.

Darcy, when he found his voice again, expressed wonder at the affliction he saw. Today some of the girls actually performed their antics between the sermons and prayers! It was the first time I had witnessed their twisting and screaming close-up. The sight and sound made me shiver. Thank God I never received my desire to be their friend. If they had not rejected me, I might well be suffering the same pinches and pushes! How embarrassing it would be to have Darcy watch me run around like a chicken with its head cut off!

When we got home and found our uncle missing, we expressed surprise and disappointment. Darcy's face fell. Looking at him, Mem's face fell, too. I cannot imagine any couple looking more dejected. What a dear soul he is, to feel his father's pain so deeply! If courtship is indeed what he is after, I suppose Mr. Cooper would like to proceed with it every bit as much as Mem would like to have him do so.

Monday ye 29th

This is the end of February, and good riddance. The wind and rain howled all through the night and flooded the rivers. It was a witch storm. Today Mem and I are staying home.

Later . . .

The weather did not keep everyone home. Several men of the Village traveled the treacherous road to Salem Town to swear complaints against Tituba Indian, Sarah Goode, and Sarah Osborn for suspicion of witchcraft. The three witches have been arrested. At ten o'clock tomorrow morning they will be questioned at Ingersoll's Ordinary, by the magistrates John Hathorne and Jonathan Corwin. They are both very important men, members of the highest court in the colony. Mem and I shall go early to find a seat.

Tuesday ye 1st of March

I could not sleep all the night, with my mind spinning about the witches. I got up while it was still dark and did all the work. Now I am waiting for Mem to wake up so we can go to the Village.

What evidence shall we see, I wonder? Unless they wish to confess, I doubt the witches will ride their broomsticks in front of us, or show us their blasphemous rituals, or consent to display their supernatural strength. Certainly midwives will search them for the place they use to give suck to the Devil when he becomes a bird, a turtle, or some other small creature. Perhaps the constables will search their belongings and find their dolls they prick with pins to torment people. Surely they will be forced to pray; witches cannot recite prayers without mistakes. And of course they will be asked if they have a familiar, usually a dog or cat, that goes about doing their evil business.

They will definitely be asked if they have signed the Devil's Book where the witches write their signatures in blood.

Later

Ingersoll's when we got there had filled to the brim and spilled onto the lawn, with more people flocking along the muddy roads. Goodman Corey came galloping up without his wife. Mem looked for Mr. Cooper, but he was absent. At last the magistrates arrived with all the trappings of their offices and their imposing array of constables and aides. They adjourned to the Meeting House.

The two magistrates took seats at a long table in front of the pulpit, facing the assembly. The witches were placed on a platform to keep them apart from the crowd. Sarah Goode wore a sour expression, as always, and met the crowd stare for stare. Tituba kept her face blank and down-turned. Sarah Osborn, whom I was seeing for the first time, seemed ready to wilt like an old blossom and drop to the ground. Goody Corey was right: The woman is just about all used up.

The Reverend Parris began with an impassioned prayer to rid the world of the great enemy of God that had been set loose among us. The marshals who brought the witches in stated that they had made diligent search for their puppets and familiars, but could find none. Then Tituba and Sarah Osborn were removed from the house, and Sarah Goode was examined.

Mr. Corwin hardly spoke a word, but in Mr. Hathorne she had met her match in orneriness. "Sarah Good, what evil spirit have you familiarity with?" — *None.* "Have you made no contracts with the Devil?" — *No.* "Why do you hurt these children?" — *I do not hurt them. I scorn it.* "Who do you employ then to do it?"—*I employ nobody.* "What creature do you employ then?"—*No creature; but I am falsely accused.* "Why did you go away muttering from Mr. Parris's house?"—*I did not mutter, but I thanked him for what he gave my child.* "Have you made no contract with the Devil?"—*No.*

The four afflicted girls—Betty Parris, Abigail Williams, Ann Putnam, and Elizabeth Hubbard—were brought in, to the front of the room, screeching and crying out as they laid eyes on the prisoner. Their fear flooded the room. I breathed it in and had to grab Mem's hand to squeeze out mine own urge to scream.

The adults around the girls soothed them. When it was quiet again, Mr. Hathorne asked them to look upon Sarah Goode and see if she was the person who hurt them. They all said yes, *yes!* She did torment them, for the past two months, at their houses and elsewhere.

Sarah Goode looked shocked and confused. She denied that she had been at their houses. She claimed she had not even been near the children. At that, Abigail Williams and Ann Putnam twisted and cried out that the witch was pinching and biting them, right then and there in the Meeting

House. We could all see Sarah Goode slumped in her chains looking angry. The witch was sending her invisible specter out of her body to hurt the girls!

Soon, Betty Parris and Elizabeth Hubbard joined in. It was terrifying to witness, and I felt a hot passion against Sarah Goode. Someone behind me muttered, "The woman should hang for this."

The girls were again soothed, and the questioning continued. The witch denied tormenting the children. She claimed it must be the others they brought to the Meeting House. It must be Osborn.

Judge Hathorne asked Sarah Goode to tell what she says when she goes muttering away from persons' houses. She hemmed and hawed and finally said it was the Commandments or Psalms. She could not recite them for him, though, but mumbled incoherently. A true sign of a witch!

And then they brought forth the witch's husband to testify. "I am afraid that she either is a witch or will be one very quickly," said he. The assembly gasped like a gust of wind. Furthermore, he added, "I may say with tears that she is an enemy to all good." The crowd seethed and hissed like a kettle boiling over.

Neighbors popped up shouting out their stories of cakes that had fallen after Sarah Goode came knocking, of cows that had dried up or even died, of crops that had withered. Beside me Mem lifted her handkerchief to her mouth and coughed into it, her wristbone protruding. It was a soft cough, of the everyday sort, but Mem has grown so thin from her sickness, every cough causes me to worry that she will fall apart.

Electrical lightning coursed through my veins, and brought me to my feet. Did I really thunder out that Sarah Goode had come to our house and left muttering a Devil's prayer? That she left Mem dreadfully ill and the chickens suddenly barren? Dear God in Heaven, I pray that I will not regret it. I beg Thee, please do not let the witch's vengeful specter come ride me like the other girls!

The questioning continued. Sarah Goode became ever more spiteful in her answers, and even used some base and wicked words against the authorities. Pray God bringeth justice strong and swift.

My hand and eyes tire. Tomorrow I will write how Sarah Osborn denied everything and how Tituba confessed without confessing.

Wednesday ye 2nd of March

I am exhausted for lack of sleep. With every itch or sensation on my skin I worry that Sarah Goode has come to prick me with pins, but so far I have seen no specters of her.

At the examinations today the judges and witches mostly repeated themselves, with very little new to add. However, Samuel Baybrook, who had to guard her, reported that Sarah Goode leaped off her horse three times, trying to get away. Ann Putnam declared that she saw the whole scene in her spectral visions.

The examination of Sarah Osborn went much the same as Sarah Goode's. Mr. Hathorne asked many questions, and the witch denied the accusations. The children were asked if they recognized her. Every one of them said that this was one of the women who did afflict them, and they had seen her in these very clothes she now wore. She denied this, and then the girls all screamed and twisted in agony before our eyes. The witch who tortured them with her specter could barely hold herself up. She sat swaying on the platform in bewilderment.

How was it that the girls could see the Invisible World that afflicted them and we could not? It was terrifying. Mem let out a gasp and plugged her mouth with her hand. I had to bite my fingernails so I would not cry out. Now my fingers are bleeding sore. In fact, when I went to open up my book, the paper did cut into a sore, and got blood on this page in the shape of a half-moon.

Sarah Osborn then declared that she was more likely to be bewitched than be a witch. She had been frightened once in her sleep, she claimed, and saw a thing like an Indian all black, which did pinch her in the neck, and pulled her by the back part of her head to the door of the house. She sounded frightened enough telling of it, that I felt brief sympathy for her. Then Mr. Hathorne made it clear that the black spirit was in fact the Devil taking her after she made a contract with him.

Her husband and others testified that Sarah Osborn had not been at Sunday Meeting these three years and two months. She protested that she had been too sick to leave the house, but nobody believed that any longer.

Giles Corey caught my eye and grinned, gloating that he had been right about the woman in his argument with Goody Corey. I wonder what she thinks now? I wish Goody Corey would come to these examinations. I miss talking with her.

After they took out Sarah Osborn on Tuesday, they brought in Tituba. The slave woman has dark skin and eyes that would please me to look at if I did not know she is an Indian. Oh, I hope the Wabanakis are kind to my stepmother! Tituba has a pleasant voice, even though it takes concentration to follow her accent. Her examination went on for hours upon hours, and I do not want to run out of ink, so I will just say the best parts of her confession.

Tituba admits that the Devil comes to her, and bids her to serve him! Sometimes he comes as a tall man from Boston, sometimes as a hog, sometimes a great black dog. He always asks her to hurt and kill the children. However, she refuses to do his bidding, even though he threatens to hurt her. This man keeps a yellow bird with him. She has seen it suck the blood between Sarah Goode's fingers. Also she has seen Sarah Osborn with some creature that has two legs and wings and a head like a woman, and they did taunt Abigail Williams. She told how the witches rode their sticks to the Putnams', and told how they dressed in silk hoods with topknots.

The more she talked, and the more she accused

the other two witches, the more she became afflicted herself. Complained she of bites and pinpricks as if she were one of the four girls. She claimed the other two women did torment her for testifying against them.

As if it did not cause enough uproar that Tituba had seen the Devil right here in Salem Village, she said that four women sometimes hurt the children. Four! Not just three? Mr. Hathorne tried to pry from her the identity of the fourth person, but "I am blind now," Tituba said, "I cannot see." She refused to speak anymore.

I felt faint realizing that another witch might be in our midst at this very moment, watching the proceedings out of evil eyes. Had I vexed the fourth witch when I spoke against Sarah Goode? Oh, how I wish I had kept my mouth shut!

Thursday ye 3rd of March

Today, Ann Putnam said the specter of Dorcas Goode was holding the Devil's Book and thrust it out at Ann to make her sign it. Is a little girl the fourth witch? I cannot imagine!

More examinations, more of the same. Goode and Osborn refuse to confess, even though Tituba has witnessed them at their evil work. Now

Tituba says that the Reverend Deodat Lawson's wife and child had been the victims of witchcraft. They died when he was Minister here in the Village. She also says she has seen nine names in the Devil's Book. Nine! A coven. I hope they are from Boston, and not in our midst. It is frightful to know that so many witches might be around, and sad to realize they can be none other than people we know, and call our friends.

Whispers are flying that the Reverend Parris beat the confession out of Tituba. Nobody questions the truth of what she says, but I am confused about two things. If Tituba knew she was guilty, why did she bake the witch cake that would catch her? And after telling so much about the witches in such vivid detail, why could she not describe the fourth one whom the girls had not named? Her clam lips make me curious, but it is not my place to question. The Lord will reveal the answers in His own way.

Friday ye 4th

Relief! No examinations today, but more tomorrow. Much work to be done to make up for time lost in the Village. If I finish mucking out the barn and catch up on the spinning, I will go find out what is happening to Mrs. Rowlandson.

Saturday ye 5th

Barn mucked. Still behind on spinning. No time for Mrs. Rowlandson yesterday, still hopeful for today. Before I can go, Mem wants me to write a letter to the Coopers and sign our uncle's name. This bold lie I will not commit. However, I will write an honest letter in my own name.

Dear Mr. Cooper,

Good day, Sir. I am penning this letter for mine uncle because it is impossible to read his handwriting. Whatever the subject is that you would like to discuss with him, you may feel free to put into writing. You will then be able to receive a response even if our uncle be absent when you visit.

God Bless ye and keep ye,
Deliverance Trembley

Now I will go copy the letter onto good paper and show it to Mem. After it is sealed and addressed, she will go to the Village and see if there is anyone riding to Haver'il who would be willing to deliver it for us.

Sunday ye 6th

When I got to the farm yesterday, Goody Corey was out in the yard arguing with her husband not to go to the Village again. Against her pleading, he saddled up his horse, determined to attend the examinations. I am sure that if only she would go once and experience the scene for herself, she would understand, and be convinced of the witches' guilt. What the mind denies, the spirit feels. But it was not my place to get in the middle of their squabble, so I kept my opinion to myself and kept out of the way.

Goody Corey stamped over and grabbed the saddle off the horse. She let her husband know she did not approve of this witch hunt. She wanted him to take no part in it, either, but he hopped on his horse barebacked and galloped away to spite her. Two of his sons-in-law went with him!

Goody Corey and I read some Proverbs for wisdom. Then we caught up with Mrs. Rowlandson, who is now on her Fifteenth Remove with a burned mouth because she was so greedy to gobble up food off the fire. Even when the starved soul can get enough food to fill her stomach, she is never satisfied. Mrs. Rowlandson makes me very grateful for all I have, though it looks like so little.

When I left, Goody Corey sent me home with double my usual handful of corn, and a piece of smoked pork besides! I hid the corn but gave Mem the meat. She cooked it in a soup of peas and carrots until it fell apart into the most savory meal I have ever tasted. She told stories of our mother, and I went to sleep feeling quite content.

The thought that Sarah Goode might be pricking me with pins escaped me entirely until I woke up with a cramp in my foot. Now I am wide awake and wondering: Do witches have anything to do with our uncle being gone so long? Did they sink his ship? Did they send wolves to attack him on his way home? Did the Wabanakis get him? Oh, how I wish we could find out where he is, and if he be safe.

Time to get Mem up for church.

Monday ye 7th of March

The day of rest was a day of stress. During any pauses between prayers and sermons the afflicted girls were tortured horribly, falling to the floor as if dead, screeching that they were being pricked by pins, and so on. "Who harms ye? Who hurts ye? Who rides ye?" people called out, but nothing the girls said made sense.

Though the Meeting House was full, a few places were empty. The Nurses, the Cloyses, the Eastys, and a few other devout Puritans are attending the mother church in Salem Town instead. There, children are not permitted to make disturbances. Goody Corey told me if it were not so far to travel and she did not have such a stubborn husband, she would do the same.

During the nooning she paid no attention to the fits of the girls, but went off to a corner and got on her knees to pray. When the services were over and everyone got up to leave, someone asked loudly why Martha Corey stayed at home during the examinations. Goodman Corey and sons had already run off their mouths to everyone about how Goody Corey does not believe in witches. A silence fell, and people stopped to hear her answer. My heart stopped, too.

She spoke something very brave or foolish, I do not know which.

Goody Corey admitted that she does not approve of the witchcraft proceedings. She does not have faith in the testimony of the afflicted children. She said the magistrates have been blinded, and she would like to open their eyes. They have lost their common sense and gotten caught up in this delusion, rather than staying the course of the Word of God. She shuns the examinations because she wants to keep her own mind under the influence of prayer. If everyone else will do the same, she says, they will see their errors.

Many a disapproving head shook in her wake as she left, including her own family. Ann Putnam fairly glared at her.

Goody Corey is very intelligent. I have seen that time and time again, from the way she understands the Bible to the way she organizes items in her kitchen. She has thoughts and opinions of her own, based on details and logic that I do not always understand. If she were a man, she could have gone to Harvard and become a famous Minister like Cotton Mather or Michael Wigglesworth. Perhaps those who leave their seats empty show a silent protest, but Goody Corey stands alone in shunning the witch hunt. Can one person be right and all the rest be wrong?

I can think of only one, and they crucified him. I fear for Goody Corey!

Tuesday ye 8th of March

The full moon must have played with my tired head. In the night I had a bad dream. I did not awake screaming or sweating; yet it was horrifying, once I awoke and thought about it. I could not erase the vivid images from my mind, nor get back to sleep all the rest of the night. For hours I prayed till the sun rose.

I dreamt that I had a baby, a tiny infant wrapped in white cloth. It had the face of Sarah Goode, all leathery and creased. In the dream I did not recognize the face as hers, though, and its ugliness did not bother me. I loved my infant. Her name was Truth. I was singing her Psalms and sitting on a high limb of an oak tree swaying gently in the summer breeze, feeding her from the little brown mole I have had under my arm since I was born.

What did it mean? Had the specter of Sarah Goode visited me? But she did not pinch, did not bite, did not torture me in any way. It was a pleasant dream! The infant was nursing from the wrong place, though. God save me! Does that mean I am a witch? How could I be a witch! I have never met the Devil in my life! Does that mean I do not love God? I love God more than life itself!

That dream felt so alive, it seemed more difficult to believe I was curled up next to Mem in bed, the same as when I went to sleep. The only difference in the world was inside my head.

A new question started spinning in my mind, and brought other questions behind it. Is it possible that the girls are letting their dreams and fantasies run away with their sense of reality? Is anybody really tormenting those girls?

What if Sarah Goode is not a witch? What else can she do but deny it, and get ever angrier at being falsely accused, and thereby seem more witchlike by her bitter tongue?

What must it be like to sit alone on that platform, being hammered with tricky questions by a clever man who assumes thee guilty? With a crowd all around pulsing hatred? Girls falling to the floor proclaiming horrors?

Sarah Goode is trapped like a beast in a cage. Words are her only weapons, but they can never set her free from the witch hunt, only tighten her chains.

Oh, I must stop these doubts. The witch must be guilty. How could God allow an innocent person to be condemned? God is Great, God is Good,

He should not, could not, would not, allow wrong to rule.

Wednesday, March ye 9th

The dream would not leave me. It replayed in my sleep again last night, except I had twin babies named Truth and Honor. Truth had the face of Sarah Goode, and Honor had the face of Sarah Osborn! Truth fed from the mole under my arm, and Honor fed from the wart between my thumb and finger. Again, the dream was exceedingly pleasant during my sleep and disturbing upon waking. I, a girl not yet a woman, mothering two witches? What does this mean?

I wanted to tell Goody Corey about the dream and ask her thoughts, but I did not dare speak the dream aloud, not even to Mem. When I got to the Corey Farm I found her alone, on her knees in prayer. Her husband had galloped off again to witness the afflictions and do his part to coax the names of the other witches out of the girls.

Instead of reading the next Remove, we decided it would be pleasing to do a Bible study of the verses that brought Mrs. Rowlandson such comfort during her captivity. Here are just a few we looked up.

Psalm 27:14, *Wait on the Lord: be of good courage,*

and he shall strengthen thine heart; wait, I say on the Lord. That is my very favorite.

Paul's prayer, II Thessalonians 3:2, *That we may be delivered from unreasonable and wicked men, for not all have faith.* Little Thomas learnt that one by heart. He loves to say "wicked men." Lisping children are very cute. That does not mean I want any, though.

Isaiah 54:7, *For a small moment have I forsaken thee, but with great mercies will I gather thee.* This is Goody Corey's favorite.

Just as I was leaving, Goodman Corey rode up all in a panic with talk from the Village. He said that the name of Martha Corey has been bandied about by the accusing girls. He blamed her for her own troubles, and gave her a foul tongue-lashing for speaking out against the proceedings on Sunday.

Goody Corey, a witch? She smiled and shook her head in that way of hers, as if she were wise to a joke. How could anyone believe such a foolish thing! Goody Corey may have strange ideas, but she is a good Gospel woman, a full Member of the church, a professor of religion. If the Devil could get her, why, he could get the Reverend Parris himself!

Those girls have gone too far. Methinks they have lost touch with their senses. If they get Goody Corey thrown into prison, I am not going to believe another word they say!

March ye 10th

Today we fast to purify our bodies for the Solemn Day of Prayer tomorrow. The whole Village will be taking part. We must repent of our sins and beseech God to rid us of the affliction. Hunger makes my head ache, or perhaps it is the dream that causes my scalp to throb.

Last night I had three babes up in my tree — Truth, Honor, and Mercy — and I loved them all equally. The face of the third infant lay hidden as she fed from my navel, which turns outward. When I tenderly lifted Mercy to pass her gas, I looked into the face of Goody Corey!

Upon waking, I felt shocked and worried that the pattern of my dream had broken. Why had the third face not belonged to Tituba? Is Goody Corey a witch after all, the same as Sarah Goode and Sarah Osborn? Or are those two not of the Devil after all, but women of God the same as Martha Corey? Would that mean Tituba Indian is a witch?

Today Mem made a comment about how quiet I have been these three days. I said simply that the witchcraft weighs heavy on my spirit. That is all the truth I dare tell her. I know her. She will never understand my newborn doubts.

March ye 11th

My sister and I have finally agreed on something. We agree that it is time to tell someone about our uncle's absence and get some advice or help. This happened because someone else came pounding on the door to find our uncle last night. This someone will not be as easy to stall as two Widows and a barrel maker. The landlord! He informed us that our uncle has not paid the rent all winter, and he has until the end of March to do so or we shall go marching.

Immediately I thought of Goody Corey, for she has a good head on her shoulders. Though she speaks her mind, she also knows how to keep her mouth shut, or her husband would have my corn (and her hide). The advice would come today, too, for I will spend the Solemn Day of Prayer in her kitchen. In fact, I shall leave as soon as I finish writing. Mem has already left for the Sheldons'.

Mem gasped in shock that I would even think

to tell Goody Corey our secret. "I will take the razor strap myself and give you the whipping of your life if you breathe a word to that old witch!"

That old witch! How dare Mem say such a thing! The way people are behaving around here, that would be all the witch hunters would need to hear. *Snap, clank,* the chains would lock around Goody Corey's ankles. We argued back and forth at length on that subject before we got back on the subject that got us started.

"If we turn to anyone for help," Mem said, "it should be someone we have always known and trusted. That means the dear Widow Ruste."

She is right. The Widow Ruste would be our best option if she did not live in Hartford. Moving here took three days, and we barely stopped to let the horses rest. That is a long way to go for swift advice.

"If we are going to send away for help," I said, "we should write to —"

"Mr. Cooper!" Mem shouted, while I was saying "Benjamin." And then I said "No!" while she was saying "Oh," and she admitted my idea was best. We shall send a letter Eastward with the next courier.

Our dear Brother,

We hope this letter finds you fine. We are fine, though we are surrounded by witches, and our uncle has gone fishing for the money to buy the farm. He has not come back for months. You know how he is. Now the rent is overdue, and we will lose the farm if we do not pay by the end of March.

God speed you,
We need you,

Thy loving sisters
Deliverance Trembley

Mem insisted on the part about witches. I did not dare disagree.

Oh, what shall we do if neither uncle nor brother returns in time? We have no money. Perhaps we could sell some of the things we have that were our father's? He liked to make furniture during the long winter indoors, and left us a bed shaped like a sleigh, a fine tableboard, and two chairs. Many houses have no chairs at all. We also have the carved cupboard that was propped atop this book.

Would that I could sell my dream. I tried to stay awake all night to avoid it, but sleep overtook me and brought me my triplets. Oh, how I loved them! — until I woke up and feared them. I lay awake wondering why I had not dreamed myself a fourth witch-baby. Why has Tituba not shown her face?

March ye 12th

When I arrived at the farm yesterday I found Goody Corey dressed in the homeliest costume: three overlarge skirts billowing one atop the other in different shades of faded indigo, covered with a moth-eaten woolen shawl gone yellow. I recalled seeing them in the old trunk in the eaves the day we fished for shoes. I did not say anything, but she must have caught my wondering look. She shrugged and said, "Waste not, want not."

While Goody Corey prayed aloud for God to open the eyes of the public and lead us to the truth about the affliction, I prayed silently for the Lord to bring my uncle home and also relieve me of my dream, or reveal its meaning. So intense was my concentration that I hardly heard Goody Corey's voice at all until she nudged my arm and said it was time we took some water and stretched our legs. She wanted to check on an ox that her husband was worried about. We walked through the covered woodshed to the barn.

The ox stood looking at us placidly. Goody Corey turned to me and said that the beast looked fine, but she was worried about me. Why was my angel voice so quiet?

Something about the look on her face, bright eyes creased all around with love, brought back the image of her as my infant Mercy. I burst into tears, and out gushed the whole story of the dream, along with all my fears and questions.

"There, there, child," Goody Corey said, hugging me close. Her shawl scratched my cheek and smelled of dust, but I did not care. I felt like precious butter melting in Goody Corey's arms. This must be what Mem missed so much about our mother.

Goody Corey told me not to worry, that she is no witch, nor am I. Nor am I being afflicted by witches. She said that she believes dream visions are simply messages from our own hearts to our heads, giving us information we need to understand and do the right thing. She said that in my wise heart I love Truth, Honor, and Mercy. Sitting high in the oak I am close to God. Seeing that the accused women are innocent as newborn babes, my heart wants me to honor the truth by my actions, and have mercy.

I cannot recall a single dream from last night. Thank Thee, O Lord, for answering my prayers and using your servant Goody Corey to relieve my spirit of this heavy weight. I deeply regret my terrible sin of speaking out against Goody Goode at the examination. I do not know how I shall ever repent of it.

Later . . .

Just returned from the Corey Farm with a huge lump of fear in my chest. Goody Corey and I were catching up with Mrs. Rowlandson when hooves galloped up to the gate. Through the window I recognized two deacons of the church, Edward Putnam and Ezekiel Cheever. Goody Corey did not seem at all surprised, but sent me into the bedroom with little Thomas and pulled the door shut. I could not see the interchange but heard the voices.

As soon as they entered, Goody Corey said,

"I know what you are come for. You are come to talk with me about being a witch, but I am none. I cannot help people's talking of me."

Edward Putnam, who is Ann's uncle, replied that they thought it their duty as fellow Church Members to let her know she had been named by one of the afflicted girls.

"But does she tell you what clothes I have on?" Goody Corey said, and I covered my mouth to stop it from laughing out loud. She was still wearing that outrageous getup from yesterday, and now I understood why. After hearing the gossip about herself, she had expected someone to arrive sooner or later and accuse her of witchcraft. Knowing that the girls always accuse by clothing, she thought to catch them in their lies by wearing an outfit they could not guess!

The men reported that they had asked Ann that very question before coming here. In suspicious voices they said, "She told us you came and blinded her until tonight so that she might not tell us what clothes you had on."

How shrewd of Ann! She knew better than to accuse by clothing. Goody Corey has several good outfits of clothes she wears in public. Goody Goode and Tituba are always seen wearing the same clothes, making them easy to identify. It seemed obvious to me that it was Ann who had dodged the men's question, not Goody Corey. But common sense is not so common in Salem Village.

The men continued to discuss the complaint, saying it was a reflection against the whole Church to have a Member accused. Goody Corey reminded them that she had professed Christ and rejoiced to hear the Word of God. Perhaps the Devil would need little effort to make witches of such idle, slothful persons as the three currently in jail, but he would never have any such luck with a Gospel Woman!

They had got her going, those men. Goody Corey launched into one of her strange lectures about how the Devil has come among us in a great rage, and God has forsaken the earth, and we need to open our eyes to what He is actually showing us instead of what we expect to see. I am sure the men did not understand her meaning any better than I, and will twist her words against her.

I walk in dread. Not even Church deacons can be trusted to think straight. I cannot imagine how the Lord will deliver my friend from this Devil's trap.

March ye 13th

Today at the Meeting House, Bethshua Pope went blind. It was temporary, but terrifying. Apparently she is now one of the afflicted. She is not a girl but a woman with children. The wagging tongues have added Mary Warren to the afflicted gossip as well. She is the servant girl at John Proctor's.

Mary told someone who told someone else who told everyone at Ingersoll's that she looked up from her spinning and saw the specter of Goody Corey standing over her. I should like to hear her accuse Goody Corey to her face, and see what happens, but the Proctors took her to their Church in Salem Town.

Betty Parris was not at Meeting. She has been sent back to Salem with her uncle Stephen Sewall to live away from the witches until she recovers her health. Maybe all of the afflicted girls should be sent away, each to places distant from the others, and see if the witches still care to torture them.

March ye 14th

For a period of five minutes in the middle of the morning, the witches flew out of mind, and the hearts of Mem and Liv swelled with happiness.

I was spinning, Mem was watching me, when we heard the unmistakable sound of strong horses pulling up a wagon heaped with barrels.

Mem jumped with joy at the sight of the Coopers out of the knothole. Then she slumped with despair because we had no meat to give them, no cheese, not even any eggs to make a cake rise. We have been eating boiled grains. Never mind, Mr. Cooper and Son never found out what a poor state we are in, for they refused to set foot inside without our uncle at home. They did not seem at all surprised to find that he was out working. In fact, they gave each other a nod and a grin. Darcy looks a little bit like his father when he grins his pockmarks away.

We all stood smiling and talking about the weather for five minutes, and then they left us a sealed letter to give our uncle. As they pulled away we smiled and waved them out of sight, until my ears hurt from smiling so hard. Then we went inside out of the cold to read the letter.

Dear Goodman Trembley,

I had hopes of speaking with you in person about this matter, but you are wise to conduct business in writing. Your hard work and clever ways have led me to hope that you might be willing to take a position working for Cooper & Sons in Haver'il. Because our barrel-making enterprise consumes ever more of our time, we have need of someone to oversee the barns and fields. As part of your salary we are pleased to offer use of a house and gardens similar to those you currently enjoy. I look forward to your reply.

Sincerely,
Jones Darcy Cooper, Senior

As I read the letter to Mem, her smile fell, then tears fell, then she fell on the bed to sob. Such misery I have never seen. I rubbed her back and searched the letter for any sign of affection toward her from Mr. Cooper, but saw none. "I am sorry, Mem," I said, and then forced my voice to brighten. "This does not mean he will never love you."

She sobbed louder.

I tried again. "If we move there, he will get to see you often, and perhaps he will notice you in the way that you desire."

Now she pounded the mattress until bits of goose down flew about.

I was sure my next idea would soothe her. "Darcy has brothers," I said. "Perhaps one of them will look just like your handsome Mr. Cooper, and you could marry someone closer to your own age, and that would be a much better match than the old man!"

She rose up from the flattened mattress and gave me a look that I knew to run away from or I would be the next thing she pounded. I do not understand my sister at all. I was just trying to help!

March ye 15th

Susannah came to tell us the latest news about the witch hunt. (Methinks her honest reason was to find out why she saw the Coopers riding through the Village with smiles on their faces.) She listened to Mem's whole sad story, and threw her arms around her, and complained how God has forsaken all mankind, and bawled her eyes out with Mem, until they both blew their noses loudly, and Mem heaved a great satisfied sigh, and made tea. Was that what I should have done yesterday, act like it was doomsday and make tea?

The sight of Susannah and Mem at the table-board reminded me of the venus glass, and I realized: Without a doubt, God has given Mem a broken heart as her fortune-telling punishment! She will not want to hear that from me, though. I shall let her figure it out for herself.

Here is the witch news. To make doubly sure that Goody Corey is causing Ann's afflictions, the magistrate had her taken to the Putnam house in person yesterday. The moment Goody Corey walked in, Ann experienced the most dreadful convulsions with her limbs writhing and her tongue protruding. It was Goody Corey, she claimed, who had covered Mrs. Pope's eyes at Sabbath. A yellow bird she saw feeding between two of Goody Corey's fingers. Then in the hearth she saw a specter of a man roasting on a spit.

"Goody Corey, you be a turning of it!" Ann cried. (Or so Susannah said.)

"The Goodwin children saw the same thing when they were afflicted by a witch," I said. "Cotton Mather described it in *Memorable Providences*."

"That proves it!" Mem said. "Goody Corey is a witch."

I had been thinking it proved that Ann had heard all about the Goodwin children and knew exactly what to say! But I held my tongue. Susannah believes every word out of the afflicted girls' mouths, and Mem believes Susannah.

The Putnams' servant Mercy Lewis was present on the scene, too, and fell into fits. Mercy cried out that the other witches were there with Martha Corey and trying to make her write in the Devil's Book. Goody Corey was asked to leave at that point, but chaos continued at the Putnam house all the night through. Mercy had to be restrained so that the witches could not drag her into the fire. It took three men holding the chair to keep her from burning up.

Susannah told the story with big eyes and grand gestures, and great sympathy for Mercy Lewis. I believe the two of them knew each other in Maine.

I am so distraught, my fingernails are chewed raw. It is only a matter of time before someone files a complaint against Goody Corey, and then the constable will come cart her off in shackles. The suspected witches are bound up tight in heavy chains so they cannot escape using their supernatural powers.

Here is another spinning question: If the accused are truly witches, why do they not hop on their brooms the second they see the constable coming?

March ye 16th

The whole Village is turning out to witness the afflictions of Abigail, Ann, Elizabeth, Mercy, Mary, and whoever else has started seeing specters. Abigail said Rebecca Nurse was tormenting her on Tuesday. Rebecca Nurse! Why, Goody Nurse is a saint! She is the head matron of a large and prominent family. She sits in the front bench of the Meeting House with the other women of the highest respectability! The last time I saw her she needed help to walk, she is getting so old and frail. How could anyone believe her a witch? It makes my eyes cross.

While Mem went to watch the spectacle, I went to Goody Corey's to read Mrs. Rowlandson's Twentieth Remove, which is her last, and very long. I was feeling sorrowful and kept my petticoat handy to dab my eyes so I could see to read.

Mrs. Rowlandson tells another captive that her heart is so heavy, it is ready to break. "So is mine, too," says Goodwife Kettle. "I hope we shall hear some good news shortly." Upon reading these words I can read no more, for I am not thinking of Mrs. Rowlandson and her friend Kettle but of Goody Corey about to be hauled away in chains. Onto her breast I fall weeping. She holds me and soothes me, she! She who is falsely accused, and I merely watching it. I feel like a humble worm that wriggles its way to the surface just in time to see the plow coming.

Tomorrow, if Goody Corey has not been arrested, we shall read to the end.

Thursday ye 17th of March

Mrs. Rowlandson has been ransomed for twenty pounds! She had a tearful reunion with her husband, and they went riding around to find her son and redeemed him for under seven pounds. Her daughter got separated from the tribe, and wandered thither and fro until she came to Providence. The governor of Rhode Island took care of her, and so the Lord brought in her daughter upon free cost.

Now that it is all over, Mrs. Rowlandson is grateful for her affliction. I will never forget her wise words: "I see when God calls a person to anything, and through never so many difficulties, yet he is fully able to carry them through, and make them see and say they have been gainers thereby." And her final words: "I have learned to look beyond present and smaller troubles, and to be quieted under them, as Moses said, Exodus 14:13,

Stand still and see the salvation of the Lord."

So now the book is over, and so is my time with Goody Corey. When I left, the dear woman took the shoes off her own feet and traded them for my holey ones. I tried to stop her, but she insisted. I have brought much comfort to her soul, she said, and she would like to bring some comfort to my soles.

Never come back to the farm again, she warned me. The wrong eyes may witness me and assume I be receiving lessons in flying broomsticks and sending my specter out to poke foolish girls with pins. Finally, she said, and shook my shoulders while she was at it: Mem and I should find us a way back to Hartford immediately. We should stay safe there until our uncle sends for us, if ever he returns from wherever he has disappeared to these months.

My eyes grew wide, and I opened my mouth to deny the truth without lying, but Goody Corey held her finger to my lips and shook her head. She knew Mem and I have been left alone. She has probably known ever since she visited our house. As long as she could keep an eye on us, she was content to stay quiet. But she will not be able to watch over us from jail — though I am sure Abigail and Ann believe she can!

I looked at my feet, warm in Goody Corey's shoes, until my shame and embarrassment would let me speak again. Lifting my tearful face, I said, "We have sent for our brother."

She nodded her approval. Then, as if the shoes were not enough, she forced upon me a smoked ham and a basket of eggs. With no more room in my arms, she wrapped me around the neck with sausages, and that was how she sent me home.

I hid the bounty from Mem. It may be enough to pay the rent if need be. That and the corn my feet no longer need.

Friday ye 18th

Walking to the shed to feed the animals seems like a journey of a thousand miles, even in good shoes. The labor of speaking takes too much effort to bother. I am so heartsore, I can hardly bear to breathe.

Oh, how I wish I could talk to Mem, but she is as caught up in the witch delusion as anyone. She is not likely to understand how I feel about Martha Corey. She will never understand why I no longer believe in witches.

Saturday ye 19th of March

Now Ann Putnam's mother, Ann Senior, has joined the ranks of the afflicted. She spent all yesterday afternoon fighting off the specter of Rebecca Nurse. The specter of a frail old woman must be a great deal stronger than the woman herself.

While Mem is off witch hunting, I stay at home waiting for Benjamin and worrying about what will happen if he does not come back in time. And though Mem has lost hope of becoming Mrs. Cooper, I have not forgotten that our uncle owes our friends from Haver'il a reply to their kind job offer.

March ye 20th, the Sabbath

A warrant was written for the arrest of Goody Corey yesterday, but the examination must wait until tomorrow. Gospel woman that she is, she came to Sunday Meeting and took her usual place. Those who believe she is a witch thought she was making a mockery of God's worship, and they were outraged.

Mr. Deodat Lawson, the Minister here before Mr. Parris, came to preach. He has taken a solemn interest in the witch examinations because Tituba claimed that the witches killed his wife and daughter, who are buried here in the Village.

As soon as he arrived at Ingersoll's yesterday, Mary Walcott went to visit him and had a fit on the spot. At first I thought it must be Mary Warren, but no, it was Mary Walcott, the captain's daughter — another girl afflicted now. Mr. Lawson was filled with amazement and horror and is ready to push the prosecutions on as earnestly as Mr. Parris.

When Mem heard that Mary Walcott is afflicted, she nodded as if she expected it. "The witches are doing it to spite Mary's aunt Sibley for having the witch cake made. That was what got them caught."

Such rudeness I have never seen as what Abigail Williams performed today. When the singing of the Psalm was concluded, she cried out, "Now stand up, and name your text!" When Mr. Lawson had finished reading it, she then shouted out in a loud and insolent voice, "It's a long text!" When in the afternoon he referred to a doctrine from the morning, Abigail shouted, "I know no doctrine you had. If you did name one, I have forgot it."

The Tithing Man did not even lift his stick! Mr. Parris himself sat there and did nothing! If I behaved that way in the Meeting House and mine uncle happened to be there to see it, I would receive a thrashing I would never forget. But the worst of it is still to come, for then, while Mr. Lawson was still talking, Abigail interrupted and said, "Look where Goodwife Corey sits on the beam, suckling her yellow bird betwixt her fingers."

Goody Corey was sitting on her bench, head bent in solemn prayer.

Then Ann Putnam joined in, exclaiming, "There is a yellow bird sitting on the Minister's hat as it hangs on the pin in the pulpit." Her parents took her arm and restrained her from speaking further. Mr. Lawson braced himself and went on with the service.

Before leaving for home, Goody Corey stood up for herself again, saying she will open the eyes of the magistrates and Ministers to the truth. She said the Devil working through mischievous girls cannot stand victorious before a Gospel Woman such as herself.

Her faith inspires me. I would like to believe she is right, but still I tremble in fear for her. How can she open eyes with words that fall upon deaf ears?

March ye 21st

A fine day it was to work outside, but did anyone stay home today? No, the whole world turned out for the examination of Goody Corey. It will be the last one I attend. I cannot bear another.

Why must Mr. Hathorne presume guilt in his questioning? It did not bother me so terribly when I believed the witches were tormenting the girls, but now his arrogant voice and superior tone make me shudder.

Mr. Hathorne did not accept the answers Goody Corey gave. He repeated his questions many times, and got the same answers many times. He does not seek truth, only guilt.

Frequently Goody Corey asked leave to go pray, and was refused. She explained that she is a Gospel Woman, and the children chanted, "Gospel witch! Gospel witch!" I would have liked to sew their mouths shut. Meanwhile Mr. Parris scribbled with a passion, writing down all that was said, page after page after page. It is a wonder he does not run out of ink.

Goody Corey was asked why she hurts the girls, who else hurts them, and other questions similar to the examinations of Goody Goode and the others. He also asked how she knew the child

Ann Putnam was bid to observe what clothes she wore when Mr. Cheever and Mr. Edward Putnam came to speak with her.

"My husband told me the others told," she said. Then the judge asked him, and Goodman Corey denied it!

Mem gasped beside me. "Can you believe it? The witch lied in front of us!"

I shook my head at my sister but did not speak. Goody Corey was not lying. I myself had heard Goodman Corey tell her such things. He is eighty years old. With all the noise constantly filling the courtroom, he must have been confused and misunderstood what the judge was asking him.

The judge then asked Goody Corey, "Did you not say your husband told you so?" and she clenched her lips shut. No matter how she argues at home, Goody Corey would never contradict her husband in public. Besides, it was a lost cause now. The entire assembly, except for me, already believed her a liar.

Too discouraged to listen anymore, I turned my mind to prayer until a new commotion caught my attention. The children were pointing their fingers and shouting that there was a man whispering in Goody Corey's ear. I saw no such man, but Judge Hathorne pursued with questions. "What did he say to you?" — *We must not believe all that these distracted children say.* "Cannot you tell what that man whispered?" — *I saw nobody.* "But did you not hear?" — *No.*

Though nobody else in the room could see or hear the whispering specter, the children fell to the floor in extreme agony and were believed.

After another hour or more of the terrible questioning, Goody Corey began to bite her lip in nervousness. When she bit her lip, the children cried out in pain and claimed she had bit their lips. When she moved her hands, the girls claimed she pinched them. When she moved her feet, the girls stomped their feet in unison as if they were puppets.

The Reverend Noyes called out, "I believe it is apparent she practiseth witchcraft in the congregation."

Bethshua Pope threw her shoe and hit Goody Corey in the head!

People around got worked up by the screaming and fits of the girls, and started shouting out stories adding to the evidence against Goody Corey. I sensed a whir of motion next to me. Mem had risen to her feet. I tugged at her dress to make her sit back down, but she shouted, "Goody Corey came to say Devil's prayers to keep me sick after the witch Sarah Goode cursed me!"

She said more, but I do not know what. My ears were dizzy with betrayal. Mine own sister had spoken against the woman who is like a mother to me! The rest of the examination was a blur. If only it were not real. If only the afflictions of the girls and the whole long, cold winter were a bad dream. If only the French and Indian Wars never happened, the charter never revoked, and I could wake up in Maine with my whole family, knowing that Truth, Honor, and Mercy still exist in the world!

Perhaps they do. This was only the examination. The trial still lies ahead. The good Lord still has time to open the eyes of the judges. Mrs. Rowlandson never lost faith, nor shall I, though I be alone in my beliefs. Alone in the world. Oh, how my heart aches. I will never be able to trust Mem again.

March ye 22nd

These days I often look up from whatever I am doing to catch Mem looking at me. Sometimes she looks worried, and sometimes she looks suspicious. Her staring makes me nervous. This morning I snapped at her to keep her eyes to herself.

She snapped right back, "Rubbish! I am my sister's keeper, and I have let you mope long enough. You have not rubbed two words together in days. Did the Corey witch put a hex on your tongue so you cannot testify against her?"

A hot feeling rushed through me. Without thinking, I flung the object in my hands at Mem. It sailed straight for her head, but she ducked and instead it landed on the hearth with a resounding slap. We both watched in horror as it slid along toward the fire.

It was the Bible. I had been reading from Proverbs.

My body was paralyzed by the shock of what I had done. I could not move to rescue the volume from the flames. Mem dove upon the book, brushed it free of ashes, and slowly turned to me.

"I do not know you anymore," she said coldly. "I fear that you are a witch, or will soon become one." She was echoing the words of William Goode in the examination of his wife! How could she!

I wished the words would flow from me to

assure her I am not a witch. To convince her that none of the women accused are guilty. But my tongue lay rooted like a stump. Mem shook her head at me in disgust, turned on her heel, and headed out for the Village to hear the examinations of Rebecca Nurse and little Dorcas Goode. Dorcas Goode! I suppose if the court will believe a saint and a baby are witches, they will believe witchery of anyone.

Mem is all I have left in this world. She would not call me out as a witch to the court—would she?

Wednesday ye 23rd of March

It was a full moon last night, and apparently the witches were very busy, though I did not pay attention when Mem prattled on about who tried to get whom to sign the little red book.

While she was at the examinations that I refuse to go to ever again, I propped the door open to let in the birdsong and the scent of spring. The fresh air invigorated me, and I felt moved to turn over the garden soil for planting. In the afternoon I dug up a bushel of tender new dandelion greens to fry in dried salt pork for supper. As I scrubbed the roots clean I caught myself humming. For a space of ten minutes I had forgotten that there is no joy in the world.

When Mem got home she came straight to me and shouted, "Deliverance Trembley, you had better listen to me and listen good. Get thyself to the Meeting House tomorrow, and make sure that plenty of people see you nodding at every pearl of wisdom in Mr. Lawson's sermon!"

He is to teach us what God thinks of witches.

Why did Mem feel she had to say that? Does she honestly question my Christian faith? Does she not know in her heart that the Bible was thrown by accident? How could she believe that I am a witch, when she has lived with me all my life and knows me better than anyone?

Of course I am going tomorrow! But not to show my face to the tongue-wagging witch hunters, as Mem would have me. I am going because it is Lecture Day and I would never miss a sermon. I am a Gospel Girl. I shall go to show my face unto the Lord.

Later . . .

My skin is crawling with cold fear. I have had a horrifying thought: Have those wretched girls asked Mem why I was not at the examinations? Have they seen me in their fantasies? Is that why she confronted me about going to the Meeting House tomorrow? O Dear Lord, save me. Innocence is no defense against the spectral visions of those wicked girls.

While I am showing my face unto the Lord, it shall not hurt to make sure that Abigail and Ann get a good look, as well.

March ye 24th

After shunning the examinations, my ears heard every detail, anyway. It could not be helped, with voices all around the Meeting House repeating the talk of the previous days.

Giles Corey had been called in and asked if anything strange had happened in his wife's presence lately. He said that he had trouble praying last Saturday until Martha helped him.

"Bewitched, he was," someone said.

Sometime last week his ox was lying in the yard and would not get up but dragged its hinder parts as if it had been shot. That explains why Goody Corey felt a need to check on it the day I was there to pray with her! After a while the animal did rise and is fine now.

"Now that the witch is in jail," someone said.

Goodman Corey had a cat take ill. His wife bid him knock the cat in the head to put it out of its misery, but he did not, and the cat is well now.

"Any creature would be well without a witch to hex it," someone said.

I also heard about the long, sad examination of poor old Rebecca Nurse. The Widow Holten was among the accusers. She is convinced that the malice of Rebecca Nurse killed her husband three years ago. Apparently the Holten pigs got loose in the Nurses' field, and Goody Nurse came to their house railing and threatening to have the pigs shot. After that, Goody Holten's husband fell sick and made her Widow Holten.

Rebecca Nurse is so infirm and hard of hearing that she hardly knew what was happening to her. In the crowd I heard voices of sympathy for her, and some talk of making a petition in her favor. I am glad of it. I would as soon believe Deodat Lawson a witch as that fine lady.

When Dorcas Goode was examined, the girls went through their usual contortions in court and showed the marks of her baby teeth on their arms. She testified that her mother the witch had gave her a little snake that used to suck on her. She held up her forefinger to show where. The examiners found a deep red spot, about the bigness of a fleabite, which I have no doubt it was. The child must have remembered her mother putting a leech to a wound, to rid it of pus. But the judges took the mark as proof that the Devil had been sucking on the child's blood to take her soul, and now she has been shipped off to Boston to join her mother in prison.

Satan must have been pleased with that day's work. He tricked a man to nail his wife's coffin, ruint a saint, and condemned a little girl with milk teeth.

As for the Lecture, the Meeting House over-flowed with multitudes come to hear the Reverend Deodat Lawson. The windows had to be thrown open so everyone on the green could hang on every word. He described at great length the marvel-ous power with which Satan is able to operate on mankind. He warned us against using any counter-magic, even to help the afflicted, and condemned the use of white magic, be it horseshoes on the threshold or egg white in a glass. Mem stiffened at that.

I strained to listen carefully and understand what the Reverend Lawson said, for he used fancy language. His meaning did not always seem to match what I expected to hear. Did he say that Satan could be planting suggestions in the minds of the victims, and not using witches to do it? If so, I do not think the congregation believed him. He also warned us not to criticize others without sufficient grounds, or ever accuse falsely, or our ill will would give Satan an entry to our soul. Of course, no individuals in the Meeting House felt these words applied to themselves.

Everyone heard him say that those who are not with the girls are against them. Lack of sympathy with their pain indicates sympathy with the Devil.

In the end, he roused us all with military zeal. "ARM! ARM! ARM! against the Devil" and "PRAY! PRAY! PRAY! for protection against the Devil's wiles." It felt as if we were all breathing a collective breath. We became a heaving mass of passion against Satan. The tormented children must be relieved of their Devils! The witches must be found out and destroyed! We must repent of every sin that hath ever been committed, and deliver the poor sheep and lambs of our Lord and Savior out of the jaws and paws of the roaring lion!

Only when the Minister had finished and my hot rushing blood had cooled and slowed to normal did I remember Goody Corey in chains, and

Goody Nurse, and little Dorcas. Innocent people, I knew in my heart, the very heart that had just been pumped up to destroy them.

Now I wish I had not come to Lecture Day after all. It sickened me to know I had been breathing in rhythm with the roiling, broiling crowd that was now set to hang them some witches, as if that would solve all the ills of the world.

On the way out I caught Abigail's eye and waved.

March ye 25th

In the dark of the night I woke to hear Mem weeping softly. It is not the first time I have caught her weeping when she thinks I cannot hear her. She mourns her lost dream of becoming Mrs. Cooper. Usually I try to stay still so she does not know I am awake, but it is difficult to ignore a wet pillow turning cold. I moved my head away and rolled over.

In an instant, Mem had thrown her arms around me and was bawling at the top of her lungs, a cry of utter terror that startled a shriek out of me. The dog barked, the cat mewed, the chickens clucked and crowed. My heart galloped with fear of what I expected.

Was Mem afflicted? Were there witches send-ing out specters to torture innocent girls after all?

She wailed and blubbered and made no sense until I leaped out of bed and lit a candle to make her a cup of tea. This calmed her enough to say what had possessed her.

It was guilt.

She had taken Mr. Lawson's sermon to heart, and been overcome with remorse over the day Susannah saw the shape of the coffin in the venus glass. Their fortune-telling had invited the Devil into the house. The lingering evil of the egg white had attracted Sarah Goode here to make her sick, then Martha Corey to dry up the chicken that laid the egg. Between the two witches they had kept our uncle away, and brought the landlord to evict us, and led Mem to suffer the agony of grief over losing the most wonderful man ever to walk the earth, next to Jesus.

How could she lose a wonderful man she never had in the first place? Oh, but she would not want to hear that! I stopped the thought from escaping by biting my tongue. It hurt! Tears came to my eyes.

Mem saw them, threw her arms around me, and exclaimed, "Oh, Liv, I am so glad that you understand! Often have I wished I could talk with you like this!"

Her arms felt too good for me to admit that I did not understand at all.

March ye 26th

Is it good news? John Proctor went yesterday to fetch his servant Mary Warren home from Ingersoll's. She had spent the night there after testifying in the examinations the previous day. While crossing Cowhouse River he ran across Samuel Sibley, and asked how the folks had fared in the Village last night. Very bad, said Sibley. The girls were tortured all night, including Mary Warren.

John Proctor was angry at this, and rudely said he would have paid money rather than let Mary go to testify in the first place. He said the afflicted girls should not be allowed to continue their antics. "If they were let alone, we should all be Devils and witches quickly. They should rather be had to the whipping post."

Mary only has fits when he is not around, but when he is there he keeps her close to the spinning wheel and threatens to beat her if she must have her fits. That is all it takes to keep her sane, unless he has to go away. Then when he comes back there she is trying *that* again.

Upon parting from Sibley, Proctor said, "I am off to fetch my jade home and thresh the Devil out of her!" I hope it worked.

Five days till we be homeless, and no word from Benjamin. I pray that he received our letter. And what to say to the Coopers? I have drafted many letters in my mind. This is as far as I have got:

Dear Mr. Cooper,

I cannot land on the right words. I hope he does not come here today, for I have no idea what truth will fly out my mouth.

Sunday, March ye 27th

It was Sacrament Day, but Mr. Parris did not focus on the Resurrection of Christ. Instead, he resurrected the discussion of witchcraft. He set up his text by saying, "Christ knows how many Devils there are in His church, and who they are." And then he named his text: John 6:70, *Jesus answered them, Have not I chosen you twelve, and one of you is a devil?*

Before he finished the next verse, about Judas

Iscariot, he who betrayed Christ, I saw a blur of motion a few pews away. A woman rose up out of her seat and stormed out of the Meeting House! On her way by I saw her face, red and pinched with anger. It was Sarah Cloyse, a sister of Rebecca Nurse. The door made a loud statement behind her.

Whether it was slammed by her hand or by the wind, I do not know, but the congregation was startled. It takes great audacity to walk out during a sermon, but the Reverend Parris had made an audacious point. He might as well have come out and said that Rebecca Nurse is the Judas Iscariot of Salem Village!

Good for Sarah Cloyse!

Monday ye 28th of March

No uncle, no brother, no sleep.

The landlord will come Friday with his hand out for the rent. I have given up hope of our uncle getting home in time to pay it. I have almost given up hope of him getting home at all. There is still no word from Benjamin, either, though I am relieved that his name has not shown up on the rolls of dead or missing militia men.

Mem does not lose sleep over these things as I do. She believes the Lord will provide for us.

That is true, but the Lord will not come down to Earth and put the money into the palm of the landlord. Today I shall take Goody Corey's meat to Ingersoll's to sell. They always have use for good food to serve, and they pay money for it.

The latest gossip: Mem was not the only guilty party Mr. Lawson's sermon rousted. Mary Sibley went to Mr. Parris's house Friday and confessed that she told Tituba and John Indian to make the witch cake! The Reverend helped her write a paper to the Church Members asking forgiveness for her rashness, and he read it to them before they took the sacraments on Sunday.

I was not there to hear it, for only full Church Members may stay for the sacraments. However, the whole Village now knows that the Reverend Parris publicly rebuked Sibley for going to the Devil for help against the Devil. He is sorely distressed and grieved that our sister's actions have caused all hell to break loose. Still, Mary Sibley has been forgiven. The vote was unanimous.

I suppose it still would have been unanimous even if Goody Corey could have been there. Only men are allowed to vote.

Tuesday ye 29th

I am stunned. I barely know where to begin telling why.

We had us a visitor yesterday afternoon when I got back from Ingersoll's: Darcy Cooper. He came alone. When he heard our uncle was out at work, he would not come inside, but consented to stay and visit in the yard, with his horse as his chaperone. We talked about the weather and the witches and where our uncle might be, but my pen wants to be out with the best part already, so here it comes. Darcy said he had a question that had been wanting an answer ever since the moment he first set foot in our kitchen. It ought to be asked our uncle first, but the question could not bear to wait another moment.

Darcy looked at Mem and chewed on his lip. He looked at his feet, and kicked a stone. Then he looked at her with softness in his eyes and said, "Mumble mumble mumble?"

Later she told me what she thought he said: "Would it be a sad bull to make cream corn?" At that, she shook her head no and laughed at him. I thought his face would fall off, it looked so sad. But I have come to understand his speech, and I knew exactly what he had mumbled: "Would it be acceptable to you if I come courting?"

Hearing those words made me feel strange inside. My blood rushed with the same hot surge that comes with fright. Darcy loves Mem? How could that be? And why were my palms sweating? Why was my neck itching? Why did I have the desire to go pull out all of Mem's hair? Was I jealous?

Well, no matter, it made my heart sore to see sweet Darcy looking so distraught. I said to him, "Methinks Mem did not hear you straight. I know she wants nothing more than a sweetheart!"

Mem made big happy surprised eyes at me, and filled her face with a smile that lit up the yard. She moved toward Darcy as if to hug him, but then pulled back and wrung her hands with excitement. "Yes, oh, yes!" she said. "Tell your father that I would be most honored!"

Oh, no! She thought I meant that Darcy had been speaking for Mr. Cooper!

Darcy looked mildly confused, yet very happy, both at once. He took Mem's wringing hands in his. This seemed to calm her agitation. With the most tender expression of love, he gazed into her eyes. My skin squirmed at the sight of it, even though I do not care the least about marrying him myself. I suppose I must have been embarrassed to witness a private moment. It was a long moment. By the time he spoke again, my skin had turned inside out.

"My father will be very pleased to hear about our engagement," Darcy said slowly, every word coming out clearly. He bent to kiss Mem's hand, but by then it had slipped from his grasp, because she had fainted.

So Darcy got permission from his chaperone to carry Mem inside, and laid her on the bed. I woke her with smelling salts, and he went happily on his way. Then Mem said: "I am not going to marry *him*! What could he be thinking, ugly boy!"

She made me so angry, I could spit! "What would you rather do, live the rest of your life as a servant because you cannot have your beloved Mr. Father? Darcy may not be handsome, but he is kind, and he is strong enough to survive the pox, and he will provide a much better life for you than you deserve, you dumb skinny jade!"

"You! You, you *witch*!" she screamed.

Enough of fear. Enough of biting my tongue. Now I was angry. My blood boiled through me and rushed to my fists and sent them flying after my sister. Our bonnets came off, our hair came out by the roots, our skin scraped off under our fingernails while the animals howled. It was a fight worthy of cats.

Before long Mem was down on her stomach, with me sitting across her back and holding on to her mane of hair. "See, you are a horse," I said. "But *I AM NOT A WITCH. DO NOT YE DARE EVER SAY THAT AGAIN!*"

And she had better not, or I will make her eat her words again!

Later . . .
Methinks she should marry him today, so we shall have a home on Friday.

Later . . .
My cheek burns from the scratches. Mem's injuries look ugly and sore. Now I regret that I hurt her. Lord, forgive me and provide me with patience?

Wednesday, March ye 30th
God bless Martha Corey. On Monday the Ingersolls gave me enough for her meat and corn to keep a roof over us through April.

The family of Rebecca Nurse has been asking

around, trying to find out which of the afflicted girls first accused her. Some of them were there at Ingersoll's and told how their questioning went at the Putnam house. Young Ann says she did not at first know the name of the pale grandmother who tormented her. Mercy Lewis says Mrs. Putnam gave the name. Mrs. Putnam says she heard it first from Mercy. "It was you who told her." "No, it was you who told her."

Mary Walcott and Elizabeth Hubbard came in while the Nurse relatives were there, and the same question was posed to them. Mary and Elizabeth did not seem to know who first saw Goody Nurse, either.

Then a man passing through from Beverly said he had heard that Elizabeth Proctor was going to be examined the next day. Goody Ingersoll said she could not believe it. Elizabeth Proctor is a good woman, with five healthy children and a prosperous husband. Clearly she enjoys God's providence and is among the elect. I have heard that her grandmother was a witch, though.

"There is Goody Proctor," one of the girls said, and pointed to the empty air. "Old witch," said the other girl. "I'll have her hang."

None of the others present at the inn could see what the girls described, and the man from Beverly accused them of lying! Goody Ingersoll joined him and gave the girls a sharp tongue-lashing for making jest of a serious matter. The girls just laughed. One of them said, "I must have my sport!"

Sport! My heart is sore.

Thursday ye 31st of March

There was a public fast today, and we had Lecture Day in the Village again. Need I say what the topic was?

Old George Jacobs made a disturbance after the Lecture. I did not hear him myself but I was told that he shook his two walking canes about and shouted crude words about the girls. He doubts the afflicted *are* afflicted.

After the sermon, Abigail Williams claimed that there were forty witches in the parsonage meadow holding a Devil's Supper. They were using raw meat for the bread of Christ and red blood for the wine. Goody Cloyse and Goody Goode were the deacons. "Oh, Goodwife Cloyse!" Abigail exclaimed. "I did not think to see you here! Is this a time to receive the sacrament? You ran away on the Lord's Day, and scorned to receive it in the Meeting House, and is this a time to receive it? I wonder at you!"

The congregation was aghast that the witches would mock the sacred communion while good Christians were fasting and praying. In my opinion it was Abigail who did the mocking, by speaking such a thing.

Why does the crowd still choose to hear the voices of the girls instead of the voice of reason? I believe that God has spoken the truth through Goody Corey, Goody Cloyse, John Proctor, old man Jacobs, and the few others who say the girls should not be believed. It seems that the girls are the only ones who pay close attention to those who criticize them, and then look what happens! How long will it be now before old man Jacobs trades in his canes for chains?

Friday ye 1st of April

The landlord came. The money went. I spent the day getting the garden ready to plant, turning manure and crushed bones into the soil. Mem helped for part of the morning, until her lungs gave out. Now I am so tired, even my fingers have given out. I can barely hold my feather.

Saturday ye 2nd of April

I was on my knees in the garden planting the peas when up came a familiar horse pulling an unfamiliar carriage to our gate. My heart lifted. Darcy's horse! And then I remembered, and my heart fell. He intended to marry Mem. And she intended to squash him. Luckily for him, though, Mem was off in the Village getting her daily dose of gossip.

My petticoats wiped the work off my face, and I ran to greet Darcy. He was giving a hand down to a young woman who must be his sister, by the looks of her nose. She hesitated a moment, looking puzzled at me, then smiled and stepped forward to greet me before Darcy had a chance to mumble an introduction.

"My, my! My dear! You are even prettier than I expected!" she said, then gently touched my cheek. "Oh dear, Mem—the cat scratched you."

"Mumble mumble mumble," said Darcy.

"Forgive me, Deliverance!" said his sister. "You look older than twelve."

I told them Mem was in the Village on an errand, and should be back soon. Darcy then introduced his sister and chaperone, Mehitabel, who is called Hitty. Last year she married a man named Hall, so now she is Hitty Hall! By the looks of her dress, they will soon have another Hall to join them.

Babies, I do not think I want any. Maybe they will die and leave me alone. Maybe I will die and leave them alone, and that would be even worse. Besides, they hurt coming out! Women must suffer in labor because of Eve's sin in the Garden of Eden. I wish she had not eaten that apple!

"Why, what a lovely little place you keep here." Hitty took a deep breath of spring air. She looked all about at the new planted rows of peas, at the fenced yard that extends from the barn so the animals can go in and out as they please, at the distant rows of fruit trees. They blend into the landscape so that I hardly notice them, but they do make a pretty picture.

Watching Mrs. Hall admire the orchards, I had a nervous realization. I hoped nothing important must be done to those trees this time of year to make them grow a good harvest! Without apples, we would have a hungry winter.

Of course, Darcy had to ask if our uncle was home.

Oh, the reality of it hit me hard at that moment. We were not going to be living at this apple orchard next winter, anyway. Our uncle was never coming back. If he were, he would have shown up by now, or sent word. He was probably at the bottom of the ocean.

"He is not home," I said, and for the first time I could find no other words to explain him away. A big lump formed in my throat. My eyelids had all they could do to hold the flood back.

"Why, Liv, sweet child, what is wrong?" Darcy asked, with great concern in his soft eyes. I fell into his arms, and my eyelids gave up the fight, and I wept my soul out as I had done that day with Goody Corey. Before I was done I had blubbered out the whole truth and nothing but the truth about our missing uncle.

Darcy patted me on the back sympathetically as he guided me inside. Weak as a rag after crying myself dry, I flopped onto a stool. Mrs. Hall handed me some tea. She had made herself right at home, and said the lady of the house kept a very nice, neat kitchen. She lifted pleased eyebrows toward Darcy. He smiled proudly back at her. I let them think it was Mem who kept the dirt out.

"This will not do," Darcy said. "Two young women living alone is dangerous enough in these troubled times, and now you are surrounded by covens of witches? No, Liv. You and Mem must come back to Haver'il, at least until it can be discerned what has become of your uncle. I insist."

"Yes," said Mrs. Hall. "The two of you can stay with me and Mr. Hall. We shall have such fun getting ready for the baby — and the wedding!"

My head is already spinning, not knowing what to think or say, when in storms Mem and blasts, "Did I just hear what I thought I heard?"

Right behind her, in rushes Benjamin and cries out, "Praise the Lord, ye girls are still here and safe!"

And so, to make a long story short: Benjamin has given Darcy his blessing to court Mem. Darcy has gone off to New Bedford seeking word of our uncle. Mem has collapsed on the bed, crying. My pen and I are in the hayloft wondering what God wants of us all.

Sunday ye 3rd

The unmarried girls of the Village had a fine time feasting their eyes on Benjamin and trying to flirt. He did not pay any attention to a one of them, though. He has his mind set on going back to

Maine after the wars and refuses to be distracted.

Susannah Sheldon dropped her handkerchief at his feet twice, and he returned it to her with a polite nod but said nothing more. The third time she dropped it, he said, "Young woman, do you have a hole in your pocket? Perhaps you should pin your hankie down."

Mary Warren posted a note on the Meeting House door Saturday evening, and Mr. Parris read it to the congregation. Everyone was shocked. She told how her seizures had stopped, and asked for prayers of thanks for her deliverance from the affliction.

It is well known that Mr. Proctor has kept Mary under stern watch ever since he fetched her home from Ingersoll's after she testified against Goody Corey. The Proctors do not believe her when she describes specters. They told her she can go ahead and run into a fire or a river during a fit if she wants, they will not stop her. She asked them why they say such things, and Mr. Proctor told her, "Because you go to bring out innocent persons."

After the services were over, people were quick to question Mary. How was it that the witches had left her alone, yet still tortured the other girls?

"The afflicted persons did but dissemble," she said.

Mary has come to understand that the girls are lying. Are they doing it on purpose, for sport? Or do they believe they are telling the truth because they are deceived by false visions? That is the question everyone is debating.

Of course, the afflicted girls had to have their say. Someone of them pointed out that the specters are always shoving the Devil's Book in their faces and promising to relieve them of pain if they sign it. Mary Warren must have done so.

What I think is this: The afflicted girls cannot all be lying all of the time. When they are tortured before God and the court, they put their eternal souls at stake. They truly believe their visions, but that does not mean their visions are true. If Mr. Parris and the other men who bring these cases to court would follow Mr. Proctor's lead, I believe the false visions would disappear. A fire goes out if it gets no air.

At this moment my heart dares hope for the deliverance of Goody Corey and the others. Mary Warren has opened the door to Truth. I do not feel so alone in this world.

Monday ye 4th of April

My hope has turned to despair. Today Mary Warren reports that the specter of Elizabeth Proctor got her out of bed in the middle of the night and lectured her for posting the note for prayers. Captain Walcott and Lieutenant Ingersoll rode to Salem to swear a complaint against Elizabeth Proctor and Sarah Cloyse.

Abigail Williams saw a new face in the specters: John Proctor! "What? Are you come, too?" she said. "You can pinch as well as your wife."

Mem despairs as well, but not about the witches. She does not want to marry Darcy, and spends most of her time lying in bed feeling sorry for herself. Benjamin is losing his patience, and has threatened to beat some sense into her if he catches her in bed crying instead of in the garden working. He says she can refuse to marry Darcy if she wants, but do not expect him to support her. She can be the wife of a wealthy businessman, or she can be a servant. Take her pick.

Tuesday ye 5th of April

Last night I dreamt that Salem Village had built a new building on the training field. It was a prison in exactly the same shape and size as the Meeting

House, except the prison did not have benches or pews. Half of the Villagers were shackled in the prison, and the other half were in the Meeting House accusing them. I was in the prison, and very sad because I could not find Mem. I could not see everyone there, since we were so many, all stacked atop one another like firewood. But I had a feeling that she was in the Meeting House.

Yesterday a Village committee bought two acres for a schoolhouse next to Dr. Griggs. I do not know who there will be left to go to school, though, with half of the population afflicted and the other half in jail.

Wednesday ye 6th of April

Woke up in the night feeling two pinches in my side, which grew sharper with each breath. The Widow Ruste used to call them growing pains. Ann and Abigail would call them witches.

The full moon shone bright through the window. I looked around to see if there were any specters in the room, just in case. All I saw was a lump of Benjamin in our uncle's bed across the room and a lump of Mem beside me.

Thursday ye 7th of April

The best thing about having Ben home is the meat. When he cannot shoot it, he buys it. Methinks the chickens like having him here, too. They have been giving us enough eggs to please his appetite for cakes.

Friday ye 8th of April

Warrants were finally issued today for the arrest of Sarah Cloyse and Elizabeth Proctor. The examination will be held the eleventh hour of the eleventh day in Salem Town, not in the Village, as has been the pattern. It has all become too complicated, with too many witnesses and too much paperwork for local magistrates to handle. The witchcraft of little Salem Village has become a large concern to Massachusetts. There will be a Council led by the deputy governor.

O Lord, please guide the fresh eyes to see clearly on Monday!

Saturday ye 9th of April

Mem came and sat down on the rock wall around the garden as I was picking slugs away from the new sprouting peas. In a trembling manner she told me I must go to the examinations on Monday.

I told her no. Never again. She asked me why not.

Oh, how I yearned to tell her! About my dreams, about my conversations with Goody Corey, about all the things I have noticed that lead me to think differently. Yet I did not know how to begin. She is caught up in the delusion, and can see no other way. If I fail to make her see why I do not believe the girls are right, what is to prevent Mem from believing me a witch? Any detail I give to convince her could be turned against me, just as Giles Corey's words have been twisted against Martha, and those of little Dorcas against her mother.

"I prefer to stay home, keep my mind clear, and pray for the afflicted rather than sit in a crowd and spur them on," I finally said, and thought to add gently: "Will you stay here and pray with me, instead?"

"You sound like your friend the witch!" Mem shouted. I would have throttled her except while I was making my fist I remembered my prayer for patience.

Choking back tears, Mem got up and wrung her hands and paced circles around the budding rhubarb. "Can you not see that if you are not with the girls, you are against them?" she said. "And if you are against them, you are with the Devil?"

Enough of patience. That made me so angry, I smashed a slug between two rocks. "Remembrance," I said, "you make about as much sense as a dandelion having kittens. I answer to God above, and desire only to do His will. You should know better than anyone, since you have lived with me all my life. If you have any doubt about it, then you can go to the Devil and ask him yourself!"

Mem stormed into the house and made a statement with the door like Goody Cloyse on Sunday. All the rest of the day she spent convincing Benjamin that the afflicted girls need us at the examinations. He insists that I go.

I should never have cursed my sister. It were better that I beat her up.

Sunday ye 10th

We had expected Darcy to come courting Mem yesterday, but he sent word that he is still seeking word of our uncle in New Bedford. Benjamin has informed Mem in no uncertain terms that she is to be kind to Darcy when he does come, and give no signal that she dislikes him.

"I do not dislike him," Mem said. "I just do not want to marry him."

That is good. If she does not dislike him, then she likes him. Her like will surely grow to love. How could a woman not love kindness?

As for Sunday Meeting, I am disgusted. Tituba's husband, John Indian, disrupted the service. He said Sarah Cloyse was biting and pinching him, though she is in jail. He said she drew blood, and held up his arm to show it. Methinks he bit himself, a pretty trick he must have learnt from Abigail Williams. He probably hopes to escape accusation himself. Accuse or be accused.

Between services Mercy Lewis had a mighty fit at Ingersoll's, saying Goody Cloyse was after her. Back at the parsonage Abigail Williams saw Cloyse, too, among a crowd of several who tormented her. Our Salem Village witches are very talented, to be two places at once pinching and biting two different people!

Monday ye 11th of April

Mem begged Benjamin to leave for Salem Town before sunrise so we could get us a seat close to the front of the First Church, but he did not feel a prime view of the accused and accusers was worth the loss of an hour's sleep. We sat in the back, and were lucky to sit at all, given the numbers in the crowd. I would just have soon stayed outside, where I could distract myself with looking at clouds and not witness the spectacle within the building, but Benjamin would not allow it.

I do not know what Mem told him, but our brother has been keeping eagle eyes on me. It is getting ever more difficult to sneak time with my writing book. I have found a secret place under the boughs of an old drooping pine out in the woods where I take it, because Mem watches me in the house and Benjamin watches me in the barn. I try to keep the book hidden in the root cellar, where I know it will stay dry and safe, but sometimes it must stay in my pocket.

After the Reverend Nicholas Noyes delivered the opening prayer, I tried to keep on praying and ignore the examination, but it was difficult in that racket. Elizabeth Hubbard sat in a trance, but the rest of the girls and John Indian had their usual fits and outbursts. The crowd could not contain themselves, either.

It disappointed me to see that the local magistrates Mr. Hathorne and Mr. Corwin still presided, even though a larger Council of learned men was present. John Indian was plied with questions first. He said Sarah Cloyse choked him and brought him the Devil's Book to sign. "When did I hurt thee?" Goody Cloyse broke out. "A great many times," he replied, and she exclaimed, "Oh, you are a grievous liar!"

Mary Walcott took her turn saying Cloyse hurt her and brought her the book. "What was you to do with it?" asked the Court. "To touch it, and be well," Mary answered, and fell into a seizure.

Abigail Williams gave many details, and told about the forty witches taking the Devil's sacrament in Mr. Parris's pasture. She said the witches drank the blood they had taken from the afflicted! And that Sarah Cloyse was the deacon who passed the cup! At that, Sarah Cloyse asked for water, and dropped down, as one seized with a dying, fainting fit. It must have been a terrible shock for her sensitive spirit to hear such a lie about herself. However, the sympathy of the crowd clearly went to the screaming children.

"Oh! Her spirit has gone to the prison to her sister Nurse!"

"There is the black man whispering in Cloyse's ear!"

"There is a yellow bird flying around her head!"

Men and women rushed to soothe the girls in

their death poses, their gasping, their convulsive spasms of agony. John Indian tumbled and rolled his ugly body about the floor. I wanted to escape, to get up and run as far away as my legs and lungs would take me. Instead, I sat still and tried to block it all out with the Lord's Prayer. It was like trying to end a toothache with a wish.

Tuesday, April ye 12th

Just before dark yesterday, Darcy Cooper rode up on his sweating horse. He said a man with our uncle's name signed on to a ship that was due back many weeks ago. The ship is presumed sunk by the stormy winter. Not a word of them has come floating back. Captain and crew are presumed dead.

Mem and I fell into each other's arms and wept.

Benjamin would not hear of Darcy riding home in the dark, or spending good money to put up at an inn. He slept on a pallet in the loft with the chickens, close to God and away from the dog.

Mem went to bed early, but I stayed up late listening to Darcy and Ben become brothers over mugs of ale. Benjamin told all about militia life on the frontier, while Darcy told all about barrel-making. Benjamin proposed that Darcy and Mem move Eastward after the war and go into business there. Darcy said he likes the way Trembleys think!

When I crawled into bed with Mem, her body shook with silent sobs. I stroked her hair, trying to soothe her. "Our uncle is in a better place now," I said, unless he is with the Devil, but that did not need saying. "God will provide for us. He always has."

She pulled away and hissed, "You do not understand anything, do you? I am not crying because of our uncle!"

So it was Darcy, then. She really does not want to marry him. She is right, I do not understand.

Wednesday, April ye 13th

Monday got cut off by Tuesday, but there was much more to tell about the examinations. When Elizabeth Proctor came forward, there were many witnesses who claimed that she hurt them and that she brought them the book to write in. Ann Putnam said that Goody Proctor had made her maid set her hand to it. I knew that those girls would turn against Mary Warren after she told that they do dissemble!

Abigail Williams turned to Mrs. Proctor and said, "Did you not tell me that your maid had written?"

Mrs. Proctor was utterly amazed. She said, "Dear child, it is not so. There is another judgment, dear child." Her kindness was thrown away on the wretched girls, for Abigail and Ann commenced to outdo themselves with fits. Mrs. Proctor was so shocked at that, she fell into a sort of trance, silent and still as a stone.

Her husband could not abide it. With indignation he rose up and expressed his outrage at the nonsense in bold, strong, and unguarded language. I wished that Goodman Corey had done the same for his wife! Yet soon I was just as relieved that he had not, for it was not long before the girls were calling out against John Proctor! First Ann Putnam, and then Abigail Williams cried out, "There is Goodman Proctor going to Mrs. Pope!"

Mrs. Pope presently fell into a fit.

Then they shouted, "There is Goodman Proctor going to hurt Goody Bibber!"

Immediately Goody Bibber fell into a fit.

On and on it went, and now the circle of accusers had spread ever wider. A stream of witnesses gushed forth, and called out a stream of names. Benjamin Gould claimed to have seen many specters in his chamber, including Giles Corey with Martha. Goodman Corey, a wizard?

I did not know whether to laugh or cry.

The few times I have seen Goodman Corey since his wife's examination, he has seemed short in stature and long in the face. His daughter told me at Sunday Meeting that she is very concerned that he may do himself in. I surely hope he does not! Suicide is the only sin that can never be repented.

He is sore distressed at the turn of events, and regrets anything he might have said to implicate his wife. He does not believe Martha to be a witch. Because he knows she is not one, he now wonders if there are any witches at all. The two sons-in-law who once spake ill of Martha Corey are now wagging their tongues against Giles! Perhaps they do not believe what their tongues wag, but only do it to avoid being accused themselves.

Apparently witches run in families. By the time the day was done, Goodman Proctor was imprisoned as a wizard.

As we got into the carriage to head home, Benjamin shook his head in astonishment. "I believe that the girls are suffering from the Devil's Hand. Still, how can it be that good people are committed to prison on their word alone? How can someone under the influence of Satan be reliable? How can sane people trust the hallucinations of little girls and slaves, instead of their own eyes and ears? Did anyone search John Proctor's house for his puppets or familiars? Has anyone ever seen him perform any magic in person?"

Such a feeling of relief flooded my body at that moment, it made my head float. "Thank you!" I burst out, and could not help but gloat at Mem. "There is somebody else in this world who still has a brain in his head!"

"Liv!" she said. "What are you saying!"

I gushed: "Do you honestly think that if John Proctor were a wizard, he would send his specter out to torture innocent people, right there in front of God and everyone else? If he were a wizard, do you not think he would have the good sense to stay home on Monday, or at least to keep his specter to himself in court, where he would be sure to get caught? Open your eyes, Mem. Anybody who dares call those girls into question immediately becomes a victim of their accusations."

Ben nodded. "If it looks like horse dung and smells like horse dung, it is probably horse dung."

I laughed. Mem folded her arms over her chest and glared at us each in turn. "Benjamin may have a brain, but he *obviously* never took it to Harvard. Do you not think that the Ministers and judges know more about these matters than we do? If they are convinced by the spectral evidence, then who are we to disagree? Witches work within the invisible world. How *can* anyone other than the girls themselves know who afflicts them? If nobody but the horse sees or smells the horse dung, that does not mean it is not still there."

Benjamin kissed his teeth, and whipped the horse on faster. Methinks she convinced him! How is it that Mem always manages to win the day?

April ye 14th

Dreamt I was flying away from wolves in the dark, but no matter how high I fly, they can jump higher, and pull me down by my heels. I woke in a terror before they could eat me and did not dare fall back to sleep. Why do I fly like a witch? Why do wolves leap like frogs? Oh, if only I could talk to Goody Corey!

Friday, April ye 15th

Had to leave my writing yesterday because Mem and Ben were calling for me. They stared suspiciously as I stepped out of the woods. Luckily I had not just my book but my basket with me, filled with budding fiddlehead ferns that grow along the banks of the brook out back. When they are steamed, nothing melts on the mouth so well! The second Ben laid eyes on them, he rode off to buy a spot of butter.

Saturday, April ye 16th

Today, Darcy's horses brought us an amazing sight. Off the wagon came a gush of children, each carrying some small thing — dishes, napkins, spoons. Then climbed down a group of men carrying big things — a great stuffed turkey, a pig still roasting in a portable spit, sawhorses, and a giant tableboard. Then they turned back and gave their hands up to the women carrying middle-sized things — pots and pans and kettles. With the way cleared, the elder folk picked their way carefully to the edge, and were helped down. They just carried themselves. Finally, two of the young men hopped back up and carried down an armchair with an old man tied into it.

Hitty came and hugged me and Mem, then went to direct the others in setting up the feast while Darcy made introductions. Mem, Ben, and I met all eight of Darcy's brothers and sisters, from his oldest brother, Adam, down to wheezy Robert and little Rebecca. Adam was the very likeness of his father, and Mem noticed. Her cheeks turned bright red as she stammered her greeting.

Becca counted Mem's fingers and somehow got to twelve! She told me what beautiful big feet I have. She wishes she had some like mine. I can see why Darcy beams over her like a sunflower over a garden.

We also met his two brothers-in-law, some aunts, uncles, and cousins, plus a whole tribe of bent-nosed nieces and nephews. I could hardly remember anyone's names by the time they had all been introduced. The old man in the armchair was Darcy's grandfather, who gave them their nose and name.

But where was Darcy's father? Mem watched for him over the shoulders of the women who hugged her in greeting, but he did not get down from the wagon. While the men were building a huge bonfire, another horse came trotting up, pulling a small carriage. Handsome Mr. Cooper had with him a tall, smiling woman and two boys little more than my age. I hoped she was his sister, but she did not have the right nose, and she set her hand on his arm as they approached us. Sure enough, Mr. Cooper introduced the woman as his betrothed.

Mem did not show it as she greeted his future wife, but I knew her insides must be flinching and wincing and pinching. Her nervous toes twitched under her hems. It was all she could do to put on a friendly face. She remained quiet, only speaking when spoken to all the day, and never once told one of her stories or let her beautiful laugh fly like pollen through the air.

How she could not join the pleasures of that charmed family, I do not know. After the feast, the men played horseshoes and drank ale while the boys ran up and down the road with their hoops and played ball games. The girls jumped rope and the women sat in a quilting circle, working a pattern for Mem's marriage bed. They invited me to join them with my needle and frame, but I did not know whether I wanted to sew or jump rope. If it were proper I would rather have played horseshoes! So I decided to sit in the middle and watch it all.

The men talked about horses and business and politics. The women talked about things of the house and family. They are thrilled that Darcy has found a sweetheart. Now Adam will be able to marry his girl, too. She comes from a good family, landowners near the Coopers in

Havr'il. I was taken aback to hear this. The oldest brother marries a poor orphan, while the younger marries well?

Somebody brought the old grandfather his stringed instrument, and he played songs until after a time everyone was dancing. Mr. Parris would not have approved, but Mr. Cooper said it was no sin. He said that Ministers who think every pleasure is wrong must ignore God to make their arguments. Miriam and David danced in the Bible! I danced with little Becca. Darcy danced Mem off into the meadow across the way, and they took a private stroll in full sight but out of the hearing of all forty chaperones. I wished a little bird would come tell me what they said!

It was not until the sun flowed like a river of light along the western hills that the Coopers loaded up the wagon and pulled away. Ben, Mem, and I set to cleaning up the yard. "How do you like the family?" I said to her. I, for one, was filled with a joy that I thought could only be felt by one of God's elect. I could not thank Him enough for the Coopers.

Ben laughed, as if I had spoken the most foolish thought ever to escape human lips. He himself had enjoyed the merriment as much as anyone, and had lost at horseshoes because he kept stealing looks at one of Darcy's pretty cousins. So he is not immune to girls, after all!

Mem looked away and knelt to pick up a wooden ball that one of the children had left. She studied the ball, then tossed it absently from hand to hand.

"It is a fine family," Ben said. "God shines His providence on the Trembleys letting Mem join it. They would like to have the wedding as soon as possible."

Mem pulled her arm back and threw the ball with all her might. It landed in the meadow where she had walked with Darcy. "You simpleton, Ben! No daughter from a fine family wants an ugly, limping, stuttering husband! He only wants me because he cannot do any better! Can you not see it? The family has been putting pressure on him to find a wife, so Adam can marry his sweetheart!" Then she ran crying into the house.

I do not believe she is right. Has she not seen the look on Darcy's face when she is near? He has chosen her. Oh, what a fortunate fool she is!

Sunday ye 17th of April

Now that the Coopers have gone home, the witches are flying out my pen again. On Saturday the specter of Goody Bishop from Salem Town was tormenting the girls, and so was Mary Warren. What will Mary do now? Will she go to jail, and be condemned with the innocent? Or will she recant, and go back with the girls to stay out of prison?

Methinks she is not strong in her faith like Corey, Nurse, and Cloyse. They would rather die than confess to something they did not do. Now that her master and mistress are locked in jail and cannot stand over her to keep her honest, methinks Mary will soon be suffering her fits again.

Besides all the usual characters, someone new afflicted the girls during Meeting today. To nobody's surprise, it was that awful Hobbs girl. I wonder that nobody accused her sooner, since she is so proud to say she met the Devil.

During the ride home, Ben was more quiet than usual. I asked him if the cat got his tongue. He shook his head in a troubled manner. "I am disturbed by what transpired at Meeting. Those girls should not be allowed to desecrate the Lord's Day with their antics. They should be kept at home, and suffer their affliction in private. What has possessed the Ministers and deacons?"

Now Mem was shaking her head. "You have it opposite, Benjamin. What better place than the Lord's House on the Lord's Day for the girls to receive the healing power of a congregation in prayer? What other way can the Devil be thwarted, other than faith in the Lord?"

Benjamin nodded, uncertainly, but still nodded, and said Mem made herself a good point. "Sister," he said, "I have been thinking, and I have decided that I take back my threat. Darcy is a good man from a fine family, but I do not wish to see you miserable all your life. If you do not wish to marry him, I will support you until we find a match that will make you happy."

Mem made a surprised noise in her throat, and whispered her thanks. The horse had stopped to nibble the tender shoots of grass growing up in the center strip of the road. Ben whistled and whipped the horse on.

How I wish I had the ability to sway people to my way of thinking, as Mem does!

Monday ye 18th of April

Complaints were filed today by Ezekiel Cheever and John Putnam, Jr., against Giles Corey, Abigail

Hobbs, Bridget Bishop, and Mary Warren. Those two men are keeping themselves quite busy at this. I am wondering, if they and the other few men who like to file complaints would stop going to the courts, would the girls stop their antics, too?

Mr. Hathorne and Mr. Corwin could put a stop to it, too, if they would just ask for real evidence they can see with their own eyes, instead of believing in specters.

Mr. Parris could stop the whole thing in one sermon.

Tuesday ye 19th of April

Mem and I got in another fight. Ben had to pull me off her, or I fear I would have pounded her to a pulp. It was over the examinations.

Mem woke up before the rooster to get ready, and tried to yank me out of bed to go with her. I refused. She appealed to Ben. Ben said I did not have to go if I did not want to. He said he did not wish to go, either, but planned to stay home and work. "If you have seen one examination, you have seen them all," he said.

We do not go for sport, Mem said. We go to support the girls, and smite the Devil. We go to know what is happening, to have all the latest news on the witches. That way we can know who be our friends and who be our enemies. If we do not go, we may well miss something important, and make a mistake that will alter our paths forever. We might find ourselves in the grasp of a witch we call our friend, and damage our immortal souls.

"Like Liv with Martha Corey," she said. "Benjamin, do you know that your own sister loves a witch?"

How dare she! Before Mem could say any more, I flew at her and made her bloody sorry, until Ben pulled me off her.

"What is this about?" he asked with concern.

What could I say? Benjamin is fair, that is true, and not too stupid, but I had no faith that he would believe me instead of Mem. I decided to keep it simple. "Before Martha Corey was accused, I used to go read to her from the Bible, and from Mrs. Rowlandson's narrative. We would pray together to heal the afflicted. She is a good Gospel woman, not a witch!"

At that, I gave Mem one more punch, for good measure. Ben pulled me back. She glared at me. I glared at her.

"Remembrance," said Ben, "do you think Deliverance is a witch?"

Mem rolled her eyes. "I never said Deliverance is a witch. But you have heard her yourself: She does not believe Martha Corey is a witch. She does not even believe Sarah Goode is a witch. In fact, I do not think Liv believes in witches at all. What kind of Christian does not believe in witches?"

Ben squinted at her, and at me. "Sister, do you believe in witches?"

I swallowed the lump in my throat, and thought about how to conceal the truth in honesty. "I believe that some people try to use the Devil's power through black magic," I said, "and those people believe themselves to be witches."

"Answer the question!" screamed Mem.

What could I say? "No! All right? No, I do not believe in witches anymore! Why would the Devil need the magic of witches to do his work when he has plenty of stupid people to do it for him?"

At that, Mem looked stunned, but Benjamin bent his head back and filled the room with thunderous laughter.

"There you have, it, Mem. Your sister does not believe in witches. Therefore, you need not worry.

She shall never become one. Enjoy the examinations. Liv and I have greens to plant."

Wednesday ye 20th of April

Mem came home sober in the face. She said the examinations were a nasty business, and would not tell us another word about them, since we did not care enough to go ourselves. I wanted to hear how it went with Giles Corey, but did not dare ask her. She hardly said a word all night, and kept to herself all morning, too.

"So let Mem be mum," said Ben, as we were eating dinner. "We shall hear all about the examinations soon enough whether we want to or not. Why, here comes the gossip now."

It was Susannah Sheldon, come knocking with her sewing basket. She told Benjamin that it was nice to see him looking in good health, as she had not seen him Tuesday and worried he might be ill. He wiped the crumbs off his beard and said, "The work around here does not do itself, but the examinations can go on without me, so here I be, and off I go." He tipped his hat, and went out to work. Susannah looked disappointedly at the closed door.

Then Mem and Susannah sat talking over

their sewing. At first they kept their voices low, so I could not hear their words over my spinning, but after a while they must have forgotten I was there and spoke normally. They were talking about what a "damned, Devilish rogue" Giles Corey is, and how the more he denied the accusations, the more everyone believed them.

Mem thought Goodman Corey had put on an act of supporting the witch hunt early on. He only gave evidence against his wife to divert attention away from his own wizardry. But now the truth was out. Nobody in the crowd had a good word to say about him, Susannah said. Well, I thought, nobody had a good word to say about him before he was arrested, either. How does being a rogue make him a wizard?

They discussed Mary Warren. Was she a witch or not? At first she seemed guilty, from the way all the afflicted girls fell into seizures when she opened her mouth. The only one who could speak to accuse her was Elizabeth Hubbard. Then Mary Warren herself fell into terrible seizures and convulsions, and between them uttered such words as, "O Lord, help me! O good Lord, save me!" And, "I will tell, they did, they did, they did. I will tell, they brought me to it."

Who were "they" — the girls or the witches? Or perhaps the Proctors? What would she tell? Nobody knew, for she could speak no more, and was removed from the courtroom. Susannah believes that Mary is innocent of witchcraft, and has been used by the witches to cast suspicion on the afflicted girls. Mem believes that Mary is likely a witch, else the Devil could not have used her specter. "Remember Hobbs?" Mem said.

Apparently the Hobbs girl confessed that she gave the Devil permission to use her form to do his work. It is not she in her own person who afflicts the girls, but rather the Devil himself who borrows her shape.

"The Devil cannot use any specter without the body's permission," Mem said, and looked over at me smugly, as if that were certain proof of witches.

Thursday ye 21st

There were nine complaints filed today, and tomorrow nine more people will be examined for suspicion of witchcraft. Besides those, the girls have shouted other names, including Burroughs and Jacobs. Burroughs was the unpopular Minister here before Mr. Lawson. Jacobs is the old man who denounced the girls with his two canes the last Lecture in March.

I suppose now the court will not stop until they have found forty witches, the number Abigail Williams saw at the Devil's sacrament. Each day I wake up with a feeling of dread that I might be among the number accused. The girls do not like me much more than they like Hobbs, after all.

Dreamt last night that I was spinning by the hearth up in our Maine house, and there in the kitchen sat Mem and Susannah discussing whether Benjamin is a wizard, because he said Susannah had a hole in her pocket. How could he possibly know that if he did not have super-natural powers? Goody Corey and the Widow Ruste sat with my stepmother knitting and trad-ing recipes. Little Rebecca Cooper stood at my knee reading from the Bible, and I helped her sound out the difficult words. Then my father walked in, with the dead boys trailing behind him, and I woke up in shock at the sight of them. None of the rest had surprised me in the least, though.

What a ridiculous dream! Yet it seemed so vivid and real, full of color and feeling, that when I woke up in the dark bedroom I was confused, and had to think to remember where and when I really was. Salem Village.

Again, I am convinced the girls must dream their visions. They see the specters in their dreams, and then recall them later, and cannot tell fantasy from reality.

If only I could dream my father back to life again, and this time sleep through it, long enough to talk with him, and feel his arms around me. Is it a sin of selfishness to pray for a good dream?

Friday ye 22nd

Something terrible has happened. Must write quickly before Mem gets back from her beloved examinations of the nine new witches.

I was out working in the garden yesterday, and was jolted up off my knees by a force to my head. I screamed in utter terror that a Wabanaki had crept out of the woods to take my scalp! But no, it was Mem who had me by the hair, and was twisting my head back, keeping me down on my knees.

"You told me you are not a witch, and I believed you!" she screamed, tears streaming down her face. "What is this?"

She was holding *this book* in the hand she was not using to twist my head.

The book flopped open on the ground, and Mem pushed at the pages with her toe until she stopped at what she was looking for. "What is this? What is that?"

Her toe pointed to symbols, not words. I did not remember what they were. The pages came near the beginning, and my book is nearly full now. I flipped back in my memory until I got to the Sabbath when we had made our marks in the mud outside the Meeting House. She gave me no time to explain before flipping through to another page.

"And this!" she said, pointing to a rusty brown smear shaped like half a moon. She had stopped at the pages where my blood-chewed fingers had smeared the paper, when I was writing about the examination of Goody Osborn.

"Never mind," Mem shouted. "You do not have to tell me. I know exactly what this is. This is the Devil's Book!"

I screamed for Ben, who would surely save me from Mem's wrath, but he was not around. "Mem, stop!" I screamed. "How do you expect me to answer you when you are tearing my head off?" My twisted neck hurt sharply, and I was crying, full of the rage that only pain can bring. It is a good thing she did not let me go then, or I may have murdered her.

She loosened her twist on my neck slightly. "I am afraid to let go," she said.

It did not hurt so much as before, and I could think again. She had my book. She had my heart and soul at her feet. "No," I promised, "if you let me go, I swear on the Bible I will not lay a hand on you."

"Where did you learn that line?" Mem said. "From the Devil?"

How dare she! Though it pained me, I tried to twist around so that I could kick her legs out from under her. She kept moving, too, keeping control of me. "Mem, let go! You are hurting me!" I cried. "Tie me to a tree if you are so afraid, or lock me into the bedroom. Just let me have my head back."

Here she comes, more tomorrow!

Saturday, April ye 23rd

Mem led me by the hair into the house and threw me into the bedroom, and pulled a chair across the door, and sat in it so I could not get out. From behind the door I said, "Mem, that book is not what you think. It is a diary. I have been writing my thoughts and feelings each day, the way I used to when we lived in Hartford. Remember?"

She grunted. "Well, if you be filling a book

with writing, then why have I not seen you at it? You never kept it a secret at the Widow Ruste's. What secrets do you have to keep now?"

I sighed and flopped back onto the bed, sinking down, down into the goose-down mattress. I wished I could sink into sleep and lose myself there, and wake up to start this day over. I would remember to put my book back in its hiding place. I realized now how Mem had found it: I forgot it was in my old dirty apron pocket, and Mem was washing the clothes today.

"Mem, it is just my private thoughts. That is all."

"Private thoughts?" she harrumphed. Then the door clattered, and flew open, and she stood there with her hands on her hips. "What private thoughts could you possibly have that you could not share with me? I am your sister! We share the same blood! We have been through thick and thin together!"

The pillow was warm with my tears. "I know," I said. "Yet, we do not always agree, and"—I paused to gather my courage—"I am afraid, Mem. I am deathly afraid to say my thoughts out loud. So I write them down."

She looked fearful herself, then. "Liv, if you do

not tell me what is in this book of yours, I will know you are a witch."

My heart could not have galloped any faster if it were a horse. My sins and prayers, my dreams, my ideas about the witchcraft, my mean thoughts toward Mem, my sweetness on Darcy: How could I possibly share all that with her?

In my moment of doubt, she pulled the book from her fresh clean apron and thumped on it with her knuckles. "Either you read me your book, or I shall take it to the Reverend Parris."

Something in her voice made me want to jump on her and fight to get the book away. But more strongly I just wanted to have the scene over. And I believe that in my heart I wanted to read her the book, anyway. I wanted Mem to know the inside of me, and discover my truths. If I had felt I could talk to Mem about everything, I might never have felt the need to write in the book in the first place.

Of course, I could not let her see me being too agreeable too fast, so I said, "Maybe it would be a good idea to give the book to Mr. Parris. Then he could learn about the sweetheart in a coffin."

Mem's face went pure white, and her eyes grew big. "You wrote about the egg in the glass?"

I nodded and reached for the book. "That and

many other things you would not want the world to see, Dear Mrs. Cooper *Senior.*"

She gasped, then handed the book to me. I took a deep breath and opened it to the first page, and began to read. Whenever Benjamin is not around, I have been reading to her, for she says our brother should not be privy to my private thoughts about her private thoughts.

When I read her the part where the neighbors all came to see her when she was sick, because they thought she was afflicted, she was taken aback. "I remember being shocked that they came not to soothe me but to entertain themselves," she said. "The people of Salem Village were looking for sport, and that was what the girls gave them. Once the girls got all that attention, they could not stop."

Methinks Mem is starting to understand me better, but we are only in January and have not got to the witches yet.

And now I must go look for a new secret place, where nobody can find my book, or me writing in it. I am not going to say where! The book needs a safe place where Mem cannot get it. She says when we are finished reading, it must be destroyed to protect us from the damning details. As long as I keep writing, though, we shall never finish reading. Ha!

Sunday ye 24th

Dear God, save us. Today at Sabbath, Susannah Sheldon went and saw the specter of Philip English climbing over his pew to pinch her. Philip English is a very wealthy merchant who owns many ships. He speaks with a French accent. Susannah Sheldon hates anything French, because the French and Indians killed her uncle Arthur. She saw it herself when she was very small.

Mem does not know what to think. She wants to believe her friend, yet she is starting to have doubts about the affliction. "It just gets bigger and bigger," she said. "And closer."

Too close for comfort.

Monday, April ye 25th

Darcy stopped by today, and said that tongues are wagging everywhere he goes about the nest of witches in Salem Village. He cannot bear to think of us living in this place another moment. Will we move now to Haver'il? Benjamin can have the position that was offered to our uncle.

Mem studied his face closely. What was she

looking for? Can she see his love there? I believe she does view him differently now that she has gotten to know him through my eyes, by reading my book. Yesterday we read up to February 28, when he showed up at the Sabbath alone. Now, looking back on it, it is obvious why Darcy wanted to speak with our uncle so desperately. *He* was the one who needed permission to court Mem!

Benjamin looked at Mem looking at Darcy, and said it was a fine offer. He said he never makes snap decisions, and shall sleep on the idea. Oh, I hope Benjamin agrees! I am itching to get away from here, away from the whole witch hunt, which is inching ever closer to home. It seems to me that escape is the only escape.

We had dinner together, and then Darcy said he had to move on to reach Marblehead before dark. Before parting he asked Benjamin if he might have a moment alone with Mem. Out the knothole I spied on them as Mem walked Darcy to his team and wagon loaded with barrels. He tipped his head to kiss her good-bye, and she did not push him away!

Oh, dare my heart hope that Mem will learn to love him, and that I will soon be bouncing little hook-nosed nieces and nephews on my lap?

Tuesday ye 26th of April

Mem and I have read my book through March, and she has finally been swayed to my way of thinking. It was the shoes that got her. Goody Corey is too kind and wise to be a witch. And if she is innocent, then most or perhaps even all of the other accused may also be innocent.

This afternoon Mem visited Susannah Sheldon and learned that her friend has been very busy being tortured by specters. Susannah saw two new witches on Monday, and yet another one today. For the first time in this whole mess, Mem is afraid for herself. What is to stop Susannah from imagining Mem is pinching her?

Wednesday ye 27th of April

We got through the book up to the wonderful feast of Coopers. Mem no longer believes that the specters are reliable evidence. There is still one question nagging at her, though: the confessions. "If they are not witches, why would Tituba and the Hobbs girl confess? And her mother." On Friday at the examinations, Goody Hobbs admitted taking part in the Devils' sacrament with Cloyse the deacon.

Why confess what could not have happened? I have given that much thought. Unless the direction of the court changes completely — and that is about as likely as the Ipswich River changing directions — those convicted of witch-craft will hang. Everyone knows this. *Thou shalt not suffer a witch to live.*

Only those who refuse to confess will be convicted, however. Those who confess it will be allowed to live, for it is believed that the Devil's influence can be exorcised from their souls. If the victim touches a witch who repents, the hold of the Devil is released. She is no longer a witch.

Goody Corey would rather die than confess to something she did not do. Of that much, I am sure. "To some people it is better to confess and bear the shame than not to confess and bear the pain," I said. "There are those who would rather lie and live than tell the truth and die."

Mem wonders, also, what could be causing the fits, which seem very real. The girls cannot be acting. I have given that much thought, also. "I do not know for sure," I said. "All I know is that sometimes when I am around the girls, I start to feel what they feel. I feel as though I have pins pricking my body, and I want to scream."

Even the mere memory of the feeling makes me shudder. I hate it!

"I have felt that, too!" Mem said. "But when I am not near the girls, I do not feel it. And I have never seen any specters."

"Nor I," I said. I told her I thought they remembered dream images. Also, they may be seeing visions put before them by the Devil, in order to bring down innocent people. The Devil would have a good laugh over that!

Thursday ye 28th

Today Mem got up before the rooster, and rustled about making awful noise, and there are not even any examinations in town. "What in God's name are you doing!" Ben shouted. He loves his sleep like meat loves salt.

"Packing," said Mem.

"Packing?" Benjamin and I said together.

"You heard me," said Mem. "I am getting ready to move to Haver'il. What are you two waiting for?"

I leaped out of bed and tackled Mem, only this time I did not beat her silly, but hugged her until she tickled me silly. Benjamin with a sleepy smile got up, scratched under his arms, and rode off to Haver'il to let the Coopers know.

Friday ye 29th

Darcy will arrive in the morning with the big wagon, and we will load it up and be gone from this place, not a moment too soon.

Thank you, God. Thank you!

Saturday ye 30th of April

So all our belongings are loaded end upon end, and Ben is on his horse ready to ride, and Darcy is beside the wagon offering his hand to help Mem up, when she says, "Before I marry you, Mr. Cooper, there is one matter we must resolve."

The word "marry" made my ears ring. I was so happy to hear it!

"Whatever you say, my dear future Mrs. Cooper," said Darcy.

"We must resolve the matter of my dowry."

Benjamin cleared his throat nervously. What dowry could he possibly be expected to give? All he has of any value is the land in Maine. He would never part with that!

Darcy put his hand out to calm Ben, then grinned at Mem and said, "You are right! We must resolve that. Here is my dowry." He plucked a chicken out of a crate and held it by the feet while it flapped its wings. "Now can we go?"

Mem smiled and shook her head. "Oh, but for me to feel right about joining your fine family, I must bring a dowry worth much more than that chicken, even if it lay golden eggs."

"Remembrance!" snapped Ben.

She ignored him and went on. "My dowry is worth more than money can by. My dowry spins, gardens, keeps house, and though she cannot cook, she can read like an angel. What's more, she can write like the Devil! Letters, I mean. And account books." Mem curtsied while gesturing toward me.

I was sitting on the cupboard with the cat in my lap, kicking the hog away from chewing my petticoats. Benjamin leaned back and sent his laughter to the clouds. Darcy looked me up and down, and tried to look serious without much luck.

"Indeed," he said. "You bring me a truly priceless dowry, Remembrance. A dowry that can keep my books! That is a dream come true."

So this is the last page of my life in Salem Farms. My Devil's Book shall hide in Haver'il, where the Lord may guide a soul to find it, if that be His will.

Tomorrow begins a new book.

Epilogue

The Trembleys were wise to escape Salem Village when they did. While Liv, Mem, and Ben were settling into their new house in Haver'il, the Reverend George Burroughs was being brought back to Salem Village for examination. By the end of May, dozens more women and men had been imprisoned for suspicion of witchcraft. Mem's friend Susannah Sheldon became one of the most active accusers.

Mem and Darcy posted their bans on the church door three weeks in a row, and in June they were married with the whole Cooper clan in attendance. The newlyweds and their "dowry," Liv, stayed with Ben in the farmhouse for the summer until their own house could be built. The farm thrived under Ben's hard work and Yankee ingenuity, and the two men continued discussing their dreams of a future in Maine.

Meanwhile, news of the Salem Witch Trials continued to reach Haver'il throughout the summer.

The first session of the Court of Oyer and Terminer was held on June 2. Those who confessed were allowed to live, while those who continued to deny the accusations were convicted and sent to the gallows. The first to be tried, pronounced guilty, and hanged for witchcraft was Bridget Bishop. Rebecca Nurse and Sarah Goode were among the next five to be executed. Along with the Reverend Burroughs, John and Elizabeth Proctor were condemned in the next round of six, though Elizabeth's life was spared because she was pregnant.

Goodman Giles Corey refused to enter a plea, so the court demanded that he be stoned to make him talk. With hands and feet tied, he was placed on his back in the field near the Meeting House. Heavy stones were placed on his chest, but still he did not enter a plea. After two days of agony, he died on September 19.

Martha Corey was tried and convicted on September 9. Two days after the death of her husband, she was hanged with seven others on Gallows Hill. Goody Corey maintained her innocence until the last, and expressed her devotion to God in her dying prayer.

By now, 144 people had been accused in court, and most of them jailed. Three had died waiting for trial, including Sarah Osborn. Many infants died, including the one Liv had noticed Sarah Goode was carrying in the winter. Finally, after twenty executions, Governor Phips decided that spectral evidence should no longer be allowed in the trials. The remaining witchcraft cases were tried in May 1693. There were no more convictions.

Liv was glad that clear vision had won in the end. Even though Goody Corey lost her life wrongly, she would not be remembered as a witch, but as a good Gospel woman who had dared stand up for reason, even against a crowd.

After the trials ended, people began to ignore the afflicted witnesses and return their attention to everyday life. Liv enjoyed keeping accounts for the Haver'il barrel shop, and soon she had a niece named Remembrance and a nephew named Darcy to keep her busy.

Sadly, Mem's health remained frail. She succumbed to a fever in the winter of 1698. Liv tended the children as her own until two years later. Then, after a proper period of mourning, she became the second wife of Darcy. She had always loved him, but had never told anyone except her secret diary.

Liv and Darcy moved with Ben and the children to reclaim the Trembley homestead and expand the barrel business. Together Liv and Darcy had seven more children, giving them nine in all. God made them two wheezy ones they loved like Mem. Their children gave them a total of sixty grandchildren, and by the time she passed away at age seventy-eight, Liv had too many great-grandchildren to count!

Occasionally through the years, Liv's children and grandchildren would ask her about the Salem witches. The memories were deeply painful to her, and she spoke little of the events. However, when one of Liv's granddaughters went to the place where she had buried her diary in a cedar box, the box could not be dug up. On the spot stood a shoemaker's shop.

Life in America in 1691

Historical Note

The events surrounding the Salem Witch Trials have fascinated the American imagination since 1692, when the jails of Essex County, in the colony of Massachusetts, overflowed with upwards of 140 men and women suspected of witchcraft. Nineteen people were hanged and one pressed to death under rocks before reason prevailed and the witch hunt ended.

By 1693, though they still believed in witches, the community realized that they had wrongly relied on invisible "spectral evidence" for convictions. They felt that the devil had deluded them into condemning the innocents. In 1697, Salem ministers sponsored a day of prayer and fasting, and asked forgiveness for the executions. During a service at the Salem Village Meeting House in 1706, Ann Putnam, the most active of the accusers, asked publicly for forgiveness.

What really happened in Salem Village? Anyone who wants to figure out the answer must think carefully about some difficult questions. What caused the strange behavior of the "afflicted" persons? How could a whole community of reasonable people believe in witches? Why did intelligent judges convict nineteen citizens to hang based on invisible evidence? Countless authors have tried to answer the questions for over 300 years, and one would expect some sure answers by now. Unfortunately, we simply cannot know the truth for sure because we do not have enough proof.

Much has been written about the trials, of course, but mostly not by the actual people involved. Most of the personal writings and journals that were probably written around that time no longer exist. Even many of the court documents have disappeared. Why? Historians believe that the people caught up by the delusion destroyed the evidence of their involvement out of shame and embarrassment. They did not want to leave a record of it for other people to find.

We now know one thing for certain, though: The "facts" most authors have traditionally given about the trials are actually based on fictions or myths. The most famous myth is this one: A circle of girls gathered in the kitchen of Reverend Samuel Parris to tell fortunes and hear supernatural stories told by the slave Tituba Indian.

These guilt-stricken girls later panicked and became the "afflicted" group of hysterics. In fact, scholars have found absolutely *no* primary evidence to support the theory of the occult circle. They have found absolutely *no* evidence linking Tituba to any fortune-telling. So where did this myth come from?

For decades Charles W. Upham's 1867 book *Salem Witchcraft* was considered the best authority on the trials. Upham claimed: "During the winter of 1691 and 1692, a circle of young girls had been formed, who were in the habit of meeting at Mr. Parris's house for the purpose of practising palmistry, and other arts of fortune-telling." Scholars who have gone back to study the primary sources of the time have determined that Upham probably drew his interpretation from a 1702 essay by the Reverend John Hale. Hale was a minister who had been involved in the witch hunt. In his writings he mentioned *one* afflicted person who had *years later* told him that she once "did try with an egg and a glass to find her future Husbands Calling [sic]." From this passing reference, a myth was born.

After appearing in Upham's history, the "circle of girls" story took on an ever larger life, appearing in textbooks as well as in literary accounts of the trials in fiction, poetry, and drama. Many of them are read in schools, including Elizabeth George Speare's *The Witch of Blackbird Pond*, Ann Petry's *Tituba of Salem Village*, and Patricia Clapp's *Witches' Children*. Arthur Miller's play *The Crucible* is believed by many to tell the historical truth, when actually the playwright made up much of the plot out of his imagination.

People who have read many novels about the Salem witch hunt will notice that Deliverance Trembley's diary is different from the others. It does not retell the old myths. Instead, it attempts to show the factual details about what happened in Salem Village documented by today's best historians. However, that still leaves much to the imagination!

The Trembleys and the Coopers are fictional families who could have lived in Essex County, Massachusetts in 1692. Their life stories are made up, but they interact with real people. Martha and Giles Corey, Susannah Sheldon, the Goodes, the Parrises, the Putnams, the judges, and all of the other people Liv describes in her journal are actual historical figures. Their personalities and actions in this book are based on the information available from court documents and other writings of the time.

For instance, nobody knows for certain which girl used the venus glass to predict the trade of her future husband, but some recent scholars who have looked at all the evidence believe it was most likely Susannah Sheldon. Hence she appears in Liv's diary as Mem's friend. The game in which the girls write their marks in the mud is made up, but the marks themselves are the actual shapes used by Ann Putnam and Elizabeth Hubbard in historical documents.

Scholars have come to agree that the witch hunts happened for a combination of many reasons. We can begin with the Puritan religion and its belief in the invisible world of wonders. The Puritans believed that God controlled everything, and that every event was the will of God. Thus they viewed hardships, plagues, even their trials in the French and Indian Wars as inflicted by God. Perhaps he was punishing them for their sins, or perhaps he was making life difficult to humble them and teach them to appreciate his providence.

The Puritans also believed in God's fallen angel, Satan, who could work evil through stealing the souls of men and women, his warlocks and witches. A sick child, a dead animal, a failed crop: These and many other incidents had to be caused by something. The Puritans believed that every ill event was the work of Satan and his witches. They also believed that God allowed these ills because he wanted them to do something about it: "Thou shalt not suffer a witch to live."

The history of the Massachusetts Bay Colony, the French and Indian Wars, and the conflicts in Salem Village all played important roles in creating the fearful, paranoid atmosphere that fueled the witch hunt. Residents of Salem Village, along with the rest of the colony, anxiously awaited the appointment of their new Royal Governor and the return of their revoked charter, which granted them the right of self-government. The French and Indian Wars had set all nerves on edge. Combined with the diseases that struck the colonies, the war had left a significant number of widows and orphans. In fact, many of the participants in the witch hunt, both accusers and accused, were refugees from war-decimated Maine, which was then part of Massachusetts.

Salem Village, also sometimes called Salem Farms, was no stranger to conflict even before the witch hunt. The farming community had to battle to break free from the mother church in the merchant shipping community of Salem Town. Even after they won the right to build their own meeting house and hire their own minister, villagers squabbled among themselves over how things should run. They had trouble keeping a minister because of clashes in values: humble farming versus worldly trade. Many scholars believe that longstanding family feuds and resentments influenced the witch hunts at some level. Ann Putnam, in particular, is thought to have accused people who had been in conflict with her family.

In Puritan society, women were subordinate to their husbands, fathers, or other male guardians. They might express their opinions in private, at home, but in public matters they had no speaking rights and no vote. Even when they became full members of the church, women spoke in private to the minister who then professed for them in front of the congregation. Men, in contrast, stood up for themselves to testify their faith before the members. Men, not women, were also permitted to make complaints in court. The witch hunt would not have happened if not for the men who brought the accusations into the legal system.

Of course, most of the accused — as well as the accusers — were female. Might women like Martha Corey have changed the course of the witch hunt had they been given equal rights and respect? We cannot know.

Women and girls had to work very hard in colonial New England, spinning, making cloth, sewing, making candles, and cooking over wood fires with food they had to grow or trade. Some historians go so far as to say that the affliction was a deception by bored, overworked girls seeking attention and relief from their duties during the harsh winter. Like women, Puritan children were supposed to be seen and not heard. This put young girls at the most powerless position in the society and may have caused some of the afflicted to act out "for sport," as one accuser put it. Because the community believed in the invisible world, many of them trusted every one of the girls' antics, and reacted with caring attention rather than the disciplinary action that normally punished mischief. However, the anguish of the afflicted witnesses at the examinations was very convincing. Perhaps some of the afflicted started acting out "for sport," but by the time the examinations were taking place, most of them probably believed their hallucinations were real. They had succumbed to the power of suggestion and also probably believed their dreams were true, as Puritans commonly did. Scholars say their behavior was similar to other historical occurrences of mass hysteria.

No picture of the witch hunts would be complete without mentioning the importance of gossip, which spread rapidly through the small, intimate community and fueled the hysteria. Most likely, gossip gave the accusers incriminating information that they credited to specters. The entire population of Salem Village, approximately 500 residents, were involved.

Today, Salem Village is known as the city of Danvers, Massachusetts. Little remains of the way it was during the witch hunt, but tourists may visit some of the sites. A cart path leads to the archaeological dig with the original foundation walls of the parsonage where the Parris family lived. The meeting house no longer exists, but across the street from its former location is the Witchcraft Victims' Memorial erected on the 300th anniversary of the trials in 1992. The Ingersoll House, where some of the examinations took place in 1692, is now a private home that has been modernized. The Sarah Holten House still stands, and the Nurse Homestead operates as a museum. The body of Rebecca Nurse lies nearby in an unmarked grave.

Today, the descendants of Rebecca Nurse and the others who lost their lives in the Salem witch hunts number in the hundreds of thousands.

The Puritans believed that everyone should read the Bible, and so teaching young children to read became a religious exercise as well. They used hornbooks, wooden boards with small handles at the bottom, on which paper or parchment printed with text from the Bible was mounted and then covered with a protective layer of transparent animal horn.

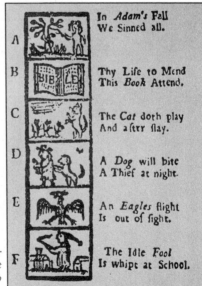

A page from a Puritan primer teaches children the alphabet through rhymes that also preach moral values.

The witchcraft trials that took place in Salem Village during the 1690s were filled with intense drama and high emotions. Above is a woodcut from 1692 that an artist rendered of the trial of Giles Corey's wife. The painting below illustrates George Jacobs's trial.

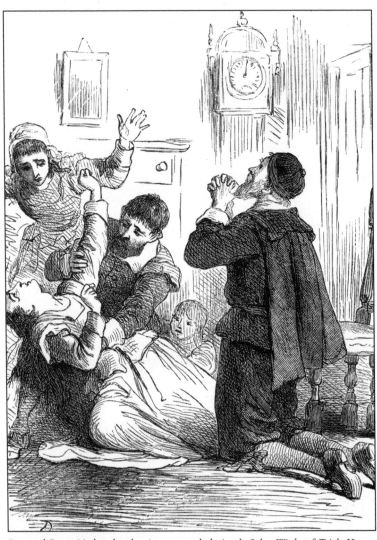

Reverend Cotton Mather played an important role during the Salem Witchcraft Trials. He was responsible for persecuting the accused and for encouraging the violent actions taken against those believed to be witches. In this woodcut from the 1690s, an illustrator portrays Cotton Mather attempting to save a woman from witchcraft by praying for her soul.

A woodcut from the height of the witchcraft hysteria in the 1690s warns innocent people to beware of Tituba Indian. She is portrayed in this illustration with witchlike characteristics, as she threatens a strong-looking man.

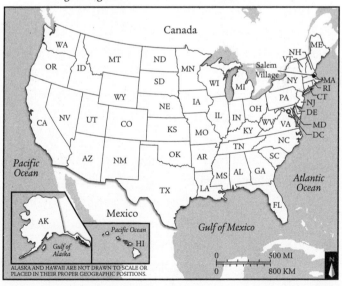

A modern map of the United States shows the approximate location of Salem Village.

About the Author

About writing *I Walk in Dread*, Lisa Rowe Fraustino says, "I have always been fascinated by anything to do with the supernatural world. When I was a child, my grandmother used to have stacks of newspapers with headlines such as 'Alien Saucer Lands in Kansas Corn Field, Abducts Cow' and 'Cincinnati Couple Emerges after Decade Lost in Bermuda Triangle.' I read them voraciously and thought they were true. Growing up I loved *Star Trek* — which was made more of magic than science fiction, I think. Beam me up, Scotty! I also loved horror movies about demonic possession like *The Exorcist* and *Rosemary's Baby*. Many nights after watching them I lay awake worried that a demon could get to me.

"By the time I got to high school, I had decided to believe that none of the supernatural world was real — and so even if it were real it couldn't harm me — but it still fascinated me. I did my senior research project on witchcraft and learned, for the first time, the sobering truth about the

Inquisition that took place during the Middle Ages. Those accused of witchcraft were tortured into confessions. Thousands burned at the stake.

"When the opportunity came to write a book about the Salem witch trials for the Dear America series, I could hardly wait to get started. Besides revisiting my old fascination with the occult, I was eager to find out more about New England's heritage because I grew up in Maine, which was part of Massachusetts at the time of the witch hunt.

"Sifting through 300 years of facts and fictions turned out to be a formidable task. It took me three years. The more I read, the more confused I became. So many conflicting stories existed. Clearly, the popular myths didn't match up with the evidence. Even the dates for the same events didn't match up in different sources! Why was it that some Puritans wrote in their diaries dates such as January 1, 1691/92? Why did some historians use the date January 11, 1692 for the same event? Eventually I figured out the reason: The Puritans used the Julian calendar, which is different from the Gregorian calendar that we use today.

"Once I understood what happened in Salem Village, I faced another challenge. How would I select from all of the possible stories, when virtually every one of the 500 residents at the time must have had a gripping tale to tell.

"Because Martha Corey was known to be an outspoken woman with opinions of her own, I decided to endear her to Liv. Perhaps, though, I have added one myth to the Salem story. In reading through the accounts about the day that the two church deacons visited Martha Corey to inform her that Ann Putnam had accused her, I kept returning to the same question. Why did Martha press the questioners to tell her if Ann said what clothes she wore? Knowing that Martha was very clever, I realized that she must have had a clever reason. Had she purposely dressed in someone else's clothes in hopes of trapping the girls in their lies? No source indicated that she did, but I believe she may have, and so that's what she does in *I Walk in Dread*. Solving puzzles and coming up with plotting details like that is one of the greatest pleasures of writing historical fiction."

Lisa Rowe Fraustino teaches English at Eastern Connecticut State University and is the critically acclaimed author of many books for children and young adults. Her picture book *The Hickory Chair* was named an ALA Notable Book, a BCCB Blue Ribbon Book, and an Oppenheim Toy Portfolio

Gold Award winner. Her young adult novel *Ash* was named an ALA Best Book for Young Adults and a New York Public Library Best Book for the Teen Age. She has also edited several young adult fiction anthologies, including *Dirty Laundry: Stories About Family Secrets*, *Soul Searching: Thirteen Stories About Faith and Belief*, and *Don't Cramp My Style: Stories About That Time of the Month*. She lives in northeastern Connecticut with her family.

Acknowledgments

I thank the Star Pants critique group—Sue Bartoletti, Han Nolan, and Ann Sullivan—for listening to multiple drafts of this book. Thanks go to my friend Dianne Hess for all of the Saturday walks in Central Park during which we brainstormed ideas for projects, including this one. To my kids, Daisy, Dan, and Olivia: Thank you for turning down the TV so I could concentrate. I really appreciate the support and careful attention of Beth Levine and the other editors, and especially the vetter at Scholastic who helped me improve the manuscript and saved me from mistakes. Finally, I am deeply indebted to all of the historians and scholars without whose painstaking research I could not have written this book, particularly Mary Beth Norton for *In the Devil's Snare: The Salem Witchcraft Crisis of 1692* (New York: Alfred Knopf, 2002); Marilynne K. Roach for *The Salem Witch Trials: A Day-By-Day Chronicle of a Community Under Siege* (New York: Cooper Square Press, 2002);

and Bernard Rosenthal for *Salem Story: Reading the Witch Trials of 1692* (New York: Cambridge UP, 1993).

༺༻

Grateful acknowledgment is made for permission to use the following:

Cover portrait by Tim O'Brien.

Cover background: Bettman/Corbis, New York, New York.

Page 228 (top): Hornbook, The Granger Collection, New York, New York.

Page 228 (bottom): New England Primer, ibid.

Page 229 (top): Trial of Giles Corey's wife, North Wind Picture Archives, Alfred, Maine.

Page 229 (bottom): Trial of George Jacobs, Hulton/Getty Images, New York, New York.

Page 230: Reverend Cotton Mather, North Wind Picture Archives, Alfred, Maine.

Page 231 (top): Woodcut of Tituba Indian, ibid.

Page 231 (bottom): Map by Jim McMahon.

Other books in the Dear America series

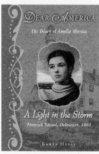

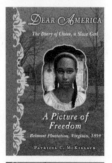